Night Shift in Barcelona

Welcome to Santa Aelina University Hospital…

As night falls on Barcelona's busiest hospital, its bustling wards transform… From the hush-filled NICU to the tense operating room, the Spanish city might be fast asleep, but St. Aelina's night shift team are *always* on standby for their patients—and each other! And in the heat of the Mediterranean night, that mix of drama and dedication might hand the hardworking staff a chance at summer love!

Set your alarm and join the night shift with…

The Night They Never Forgot by Scarlet Wilson

Their Barcelona Baby Bombshell by Traci Douglass

Their Marriage Worth Fighting For by Louisa Heaton

From Wedding Guest to Bride? by Tina Beckett

Dear Reader,

I wrote *Their Barcelona Baby Bombshell* in the autumn, when things here in the US were winding down and the weather was turning colder. So being able to escape to sunny, gorgeous Barcelona for a few hours each day was pure bliss. And delving into Carlos and Isabella's love story and baggage was super fun as well. I learned so much about Cuba and Barcelona and surfing while researching this book, and I hope my joy comes through in the story. As someone who adores Art Nouveau, getting to set scenes at some of the city's world-famous Gaudí architectural wonders was a dream come true. And Carlos is such a sweet, caring, strong, supportive hero that he was a complete pleasure to write.

I do hope you'll enjoy reading about Carlos and Isabella's journey to love and the bumps (and surprises) they encounter along the way, as well as the rest of the wonderful stories in our summer continuity set at the fictional St. Aelina's. This story was a pleasure to write, and who knows, maybe someday I'll get to visit the wonderful city of Barcelona myself. It's definitely on my bucket list!

Until next time, happy reading!

Traci <3

THEIR BARCELONA BABY BOMBSHELL

TRACI DOUGLASS

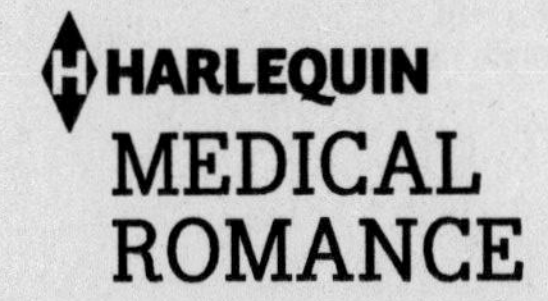

Special thanks and acknowledgement are given to Traci Douglass for her contribution to the Night Shift in Barcelona miniseries.

Recycling programs for this product may not exist in your area.

ISBN-13: 978-1-335-73721-2

Their Barcelona Baby Bombshell

For questions and comments about the quality of this book, please contact us at CustomerService@Harlequin.com.

Harlequin Enterprises ULC
22 Adelaide St. West, 41st Floor
Toronto, Ontario M5H 4E3, Canada
www.Harlequin.com

Printed in U.S.A.

Traci Douglass is a *USA TODAY* bestselling romance author with Harlequin, Entangled Publishing and Tule Publishing, and has an MFA in Writing Popular Fiction from Seton Hill University. She writes sometimes funny, usually awkward, always emotional stories about strong, quirky, wounded characters overcoming past adversity to find their forever person. Heartfelt, healing happily-ever-afters. Connect with her through her website: tracidouglassbooks.com.

Books by Traci Douglass

Harlequin Medical Romance

First Response in Florida

The Vet's Unexpected Hero
Her One-Night Secret

Finding Her Forever Family
A Mistletoe Kiss for the Single Dad
A Weekend with Her Fake Fiancé
Their Hot Hawaiian Fling
Neurosurgeon's Christmas to Remember
Costa Rican Fling with the Doc
Island Reunion with the Single Dad

Visit the Author Profile page at Harlequin.com.

To my writing sprint group for all the support and ideas and laughter. Completing two books in four months is a LOT, and I wouldn't be here and still sane without you all!

To my wonderful editor, Charlotte, who always knows exactly what needs fixed to make my books better and tells me in such a kind, helpful, supportive way.

To my awesome agent, Jill, who has talked me down from the ledge more than once so far and who continues to have my back.

To my new writing "partner," Karley, a fluffy, furry ball of love and energy who never fails to make me smile. Love you, puppers!

And to everyone who picks up one of my books. You are the reason I do what I do, and I feel so lucky and blessed and grateful every single day to have the opportunity to create stories you want to read.

Thank you!

Praise for
Traci Douglass

"*Their Hot Hawaiian Fling* by Traci Douglass is a fantastic romance.... I love this author's medical romance books and this is no exception. Both characters are well written, complex, flawed and well fleshed out. The story was perfectly paced. A great romance I highly recommend."

—*Goodreads*

PROLOGUE

April

EVENING GLASS-OFF had arrived.

Isabella Rivas dug her toes into the still-warm sand of Playa de Bogatell and stared at the gorgeous sunset, the horizon streaked with vivid oranges and pinks and purples. This was her favorite time of day—when the Barcelona tourists had cleared out and the wind and waves had died down. Water smooth enough to skate on. So quiet and peaceful and…

"Help!" a woman cried from down the beach. "Help! My husband!"

Dropping her surfboard to the sand, Isabella sprinted toward the woman. "*Señora, qué pasa?*"

The woman, white as a ghost and frantic, waved her hands at Isabella, saying in a British accent, "I don't speak Spanish. Please, you must help my husband. He's drowning out there!"

"Got it, ma'am," Isabella said, switching to English as she raced for the water. "I'll get him in. Let the lifeguards know!"

She ran into the shallows, then dived into the deeper water just beyond the sandbar, swimming hard in the direction the woman pointed. Black water surrounded her in the night, the neon red of the bobbing buoy ahead glowing like a beacon in the shadows. As her head surfaced between strokes, she spotted a vague white blob on the surface, and her adrenaline skyrocketed. In her periphery another person swam in the same direction. Too soon for the lifeguards on shore to catch up.

"Sir!" she yelled, treading water as she reached the man. "Sir! Can you hear me?"

No response.

His complexion was gray and lips bluish, and Isabella knew from her years as a paramedic that things were not good. Impossible to know exactly what had caused this, but one thing was clear—the man wasn't breathing.

"What can I do to help?" an accented male voice asked from beside her.

"Help me get him to shore, then he's going to need CPR." Isabella got on one side of the man, supporting his head while the other guy took the man's other side, and together they got the victim to dry land. The lifeguards met them there with a medical kit, and Isabella quickly told them who she was and what she needed while the Good Samaritan who'd joined her in the water began chest compressions. He seemed competent—more than competent—which was handy.

"My name's Isabella Rivas. I'm a licensed paramedic with Ambulancias Lázaro. We found this man unresponsive in the water by the buoy there, and he needed immediate medical attention." She turned to the man doing CPR. "Does he have a pulse? Respirations?"

"No," the man said, his focus on the patient. "Still nonresponsive."

"Do you have a portable defibrillator?" she asked the lifeguards in Catalan, the local dialect. "Call 061 now, please!"

One of the lifeguards pulled the machine out from their medical pack while the other went to comfort the frantic spouse and call emergency services. Isabella grabbed a nearby towel to dry the victim's chest before attaching the sticky defibrillator pads while the man across from her continued his compressions. Their eyes met briefly, his dark and chocolate brown, and she absently registered he was handsome, but now wasn't the time.

Once the pads were in place, she turned to the machine and pushed the button to cue it up. When the light came on and it beeped, she yelled, "Clear!"

The man across from her immediately lifted his hands away and scooted back, as if it was second nature. Isabella pushed the button, sending a jolt of current to the man's stopped heart. His body jerked but then returned to stillness.

"Any cardiac signs yet?" she asked as the other man pressed his fingers to the victim's carotid.

He shook his head. "No."

"Right." She readied the machine again and hit the button. The man's body jerked again, then flopped back onto the sand. His color turned grayer, and Isabella didn't like the look of it. In the distance, sirens wailed. Help was on the way, thank goodness. Whether the man had drowned or had a cardiac arrest, he needed to get to a hospital ASAP or he'd be dead. She cast the machine aside and took over compressions from the man to avoid tiring him out. He moved to the air bag the lifeguard had attached to a mask over the victim's nose and mouth to help him breathe. They got into a rhythm then, her with the compressions and him with the breaths, like they'd been working as a team for years. Nice to have someone she could depend on.

Eventually, the ambulance arrived, and Isabella turned the case over to her colleagues, giving them a rundown of how she'd found the man and what they'd done to assist him up to that point. The victim now had a faint pulse and breathed on his own and responded to calls, though mostly incoherently. Isabella guessed cardiac arrest, because of the still, smooth water. There were still rip currents, but none really to speak of where they'd found the man. For treatment they were taking him to St. Aelina's, the new, state-of-the-art training hospital nearby, so he was in good hands.

As she watched the ambulance pull away and the lifeguards return to their post tower, the mystery man beside her finally introduced himself.

"Carlos Martinez," he said. From his dark good looks, she'd say Spanish, but his accent wasn't local. "Good work on that victim."

"Same to you," she said, shaking his hand, doing her best not to glance down at his, tanned and toned almost-naked torso. "Isabella Rivas. Where are you from?"

His grin grew wider, his teeth white and straight in the gathering darkness. "Havana, Cuba. I just moved to Barcelona recently."

"Well, *benvingut a la meva Ciutat*," she said in Catalan, then chuckled at his slightly confused look. The local dialect wasn't much different from regular Spanish, but considering most people spoke Cubano, a form of the language, in his homeland, it made translation unnecessary, especially since they both had spoken English during the rescue. She laughed then smiled at him. "Welcome to my city."

He nodded, his widening smile doing all sorts of naughty things inside her.

Whoa.

Romance wasn't on her to-do list. She loved a good rom com with a happily-ever-after as much as the next person, but after spending years taking care of everyone else in her family, this time now was just for her.

Even with her off-the-charts attraction to this guy. And it wasn't just his gorgeousness that drew her to him. It was the cool, calm proficiency he'd shown during the rescue. She had a thing for men who knew what they were doing at work and at play, and this guy had *competency* written all over him.

"So, Isabella Rivas," Carlos said as they started walking back to where her surfboard still rested in the sand. "Would you like to get a drink? I know I could sure use one."

Taken aback a bit, she was glad to be bending over to pick up her surfboard so he couldn't see her face. Her cheeks were hot, and her heart slammed against her rib cage like she was a besotted teen instead of an independent thirty-four-year-old woman. She took her time getting the board, tossing her long, damp dark brown braid over her shoulder before straightening. Normally, she'd tell him she wasn't interested and be done with it. But she *was* interested. More than she should be. One drink. What would it hurt? Besides, she could use a drink to ease her adrenaline buzz from earlier, otherwise she'd never get to sleep tonight, and she had a shift in the morning.

"Fine," she said, turning back to him, the chemistry crackling around them like fireworks. "There's a bar just up the way. Good food, reasonable prices. Want to go there?"

Carlos bowed slightly, giving her a view of the rippling muscles in his broad shoulders and upper back, and her mouth definitely didn't start watering. "Whatever you desire."

What she suddenly desired was to climb him like a tree, but that thought only unsettled her more.

Down, girl. Down.

She wasn't like this. She never flirted or threw herself at guys, but something about Carlos made her melt inside. She swallowed hard past the lump of rising lust in her throat and flashed him a wobbly smile. "Great. This way, then."

Isabella stowed her surfboard in one of the lockers nearby, then joined him again on the boardwalk.

"Do you come to Bogatell Beach often?" he asked. "You obviously like surfing."

"I do." She smiled, looking straight ahead and not at him, for fear she'd do something nuts—like kiss him or something. Seriously. She needed to get over this…whatever this was. Talking about surfing helped. Surfing always calmed her. Her go-to destressor. "I like it because it's quieter. Less tourists. The waves aren't great here usually, but every once in a while you can catch some good ones. And it's close to where I live."

"Interesting," he said, frowning slightly.

"Some other locals I met in my uncle's bar talked about a place called Killers for surfing. They said it's kind of a secret."

She chuckled. "Yeah, I've gone there, too, several times, and the name suits it. Good action, but sometimes after work, I just want to relax and get away from people, you know?"

"I do." He grinned. "I hope I'm not intruding tonight."

"Not at all," she said, and surprisingly, she meant it. There was an ease about him that helped calm her. "You said your uncle owns a bar here? Which one?"

"Encanteri," he said. "Ever heard of it?"

"Absolutely. It's one of the hottest nightspots in town." She and some of her friends had been trying to get in there for months, but the lines were terrible. It would likely only get worse with summer on the way and the tourist rushing to the city. "Maybe I've got an in then, with you."

"Maybe you do." He met her gaze and held it a fraction longer than normal, and her pulse stuttered.

Oh, boy.

"Uh…" Isabella said, fumbling her words and her footsteps, getting her flip-flops tangled and nearly tripping. Thankfully, Carlos steadied her with a hand on her arm to keep her from face-planting on the boardwalk. Zings of fresh awareness stormed through her nervous system from their point of contact. "The, um, bar is just over there."

Isabella pointed to a glowing neon sign for El Chiringuito. Nothing fancy, but the food was good and the service excellent. They got an umbrella-covered table out on the deck overlooking the beach and the ocean beyond and placed their orders.

"So," Carlos said, once the server had brought their drinks—cava for her, sangria for him. "You said this beach is close to where you live?" She gave him a look, and he laughed. "Not trying to be a creeper. Honest. Just making chitchat. I want to know more about you, Isabella. You intrigue me."

She was intrigued, too. Way more than she should be. He was just so charming and nice, and low-key. In her job, she needed good radar for deceit and shady characters, and she got no weird vibes at all. Carlos seemed just what he said—a newly arrived expat from Cuba, looking to find his way in Barcelona. She found it completely endearing and disarming. Still, she wasn't an idiot. She wasn't giving some random stranger her address, no matter how hot.

"I live in El Poulenou," she said, taking a sip of her pink sparkling wine. The bubbles tickled her nose. "And you?"

"I'm actually living above my uncle's bar at the moment." Carlos watched her over the rim of his glass. "He's the one who convinced me to move to Spain in the first place. It's a nice flat, some might even say luxurious—at least by city standards."

"Nice." She smiled. "Is your uncle your only family here?"

Carlos's smile faded. He set his glass down on the table, his dark brows knit. "He's my only family period."

"Oh." She gulped more wine, the alcohol swirling nicely in her empty stomach, loosening her inhibitions slightly. "I'm sorry. Didn't mean to touch a sore spot." She sighed and sat back, letting her walls down a bit. "There were times when I wished my family would go away."

He gave a surprised snort. "That doesn't sound good."

She waved dismissively. "Oh, I don't really mean it. It's just hard, because I'm the oldest of six kids and ended up taking care of my younger siblings most of the time after my mom passed away when I was thirteen. My dad got sick shortly thereafter, too."

"Ouch. I'm sorry," he said, repeating her words from earlier. He leaned closer over the table, close enough for her to see the tiny flecks of gold in his brown eyes. Such nice, kind eyes. "Must've been really hard on you, taking on so much so young."

Rather than answer, she just nodded, grateful when their shared order of the bar's famous nachos arrived, smelling amazing. They each dished up a portion and ate.

"Anyway," she continued after devouring a mouthful of cheesy, spicy goodness, "one of the reasons I moved to Barcelona was to get away from my siblings once they were all grown and gone." She laughed. "Ironically, though, my younger brother Diego followed me here. In fact, he works at one of the local hospitals nearby, so I see him all the time now on my ambulance runs."

Carlos chuckled. "Funny how fate works out sometimes, huh?"

"Yeah," she said, looking up, their gazes tangling again. A tiny dot of cheese clung to the corner of his mouth, and Isabella licked her lips, imagining licking it off him instead.

A wild, reckless sense of excitement had taken hold of her now, one she hadn't felt in a long time. Too long. From the twinkle in his dark eyes, Carlos felt the same.

It was ridiculous. Silly. And so on.

They had barely spoken a word about anything beyond dinner, but from the casual way his leg kept brushing against hers under the table, they'd be going to bed together. Nothing long-term, nothing more than a one-night stand. Light, fun, no strings attached. Just two lonely strangers enjoying a sudden connection and a moment together. Isabella couldn't wait to get him alone.

Beneath the table, she slipped her foot out of her flip-flop and slowly ran her toes up the inside of his bare ankle, loving the way he shivered beneath her light touch. Oh, yeah. This was happening. Her widening grin matched his own. "Yes. Funny how fate works sometimes."

CHAPTER ONE

June

"BP NINETY OVER sixty-eight. Low, but holding steady. O_2 sats normal," Isabella said, holding an oxygen mask to the face of a car accident victim as the ambulance rig rumbled toward Santa Aelina's University Hospital. The young kid, still just a teenager, really, at nineteen, blinked up at her, his face pale beneath his tan, fear making his dark eyes wide and frantic-looking. "It's okay. You're going to be okay, yeah?"

The kid swallowed hard, then winced, his chest contusions and broken ribs from the vehicle rollover obviously making any movement painful. Honestly, he was lucky to be alive, considering the state of the car they'd pulled him out of, but she wouldn't tell him that. Leave it to the police, who'd question him and take a report of the accident after the medical personnel patched the kid up and released him from the ER.

Isabella glanced out the window across from her at the sunny blue evening skies. Too bad the surf wasn't so good right now. She could've used some time in the water after the day she'd had. Nothing particularly bad had happened, but she just didn't feel great. Hadn't felt great for about a week or so now, truthfully. Probably the flu bug that had been going around.

She'd started a night shift, too. Her first in a month and…ugh.

Maybe when she got off work in the morning, if it was still this nice, she'd go for a swim anyway. Early, before all the tourists hit the beach. Not the same kind of high she got from riding the perfect wave, but it would help.

Her EMT colleague drove down the ramp to the ambulance bay at St. Aelina's, then jerked to a stop before the automatic doors. Mario got out and jogged around the back to open the doors, then he and Isabella lowered the patient's gurney down to the ground and wheeled him in through to where one of the ER docs waited for them, along with a couple of nurses and techs.

"*Resum per favor,*" the female doctor said from behind her mask. *Rundown, please.*

"*Si,*" Isabella said, wheeling the gurney down the brightly lit hall toward an open trauma bay along with Mario. She listed off the patient's vitals and the facts of the accident they had so far. Once they reached the trauma bay, she and Mario assisted the nurses to transfer the patient to the hospital bed. From across the bed, her eyes locked with one of the nurses', and they seemed… familiar somehow. Warm brown with flecks of gold and… Her pulse stumbled. Oh, God.

Carlos.

After their one passionate night together, they'd both gone their separate ways. She'd never thought she'd see him again, and yet here he was. Working in the same ER where she did many runs. Where she'd see her one-night stand on pretty much a daily basis.

Perfect.

Her crap day notched lower into dumpster-fire territory. She already felt rough as hell. This wasn't improving anything. Not at all.

Never mind the traitorous fizz of unwanted excitement bubbling up inside her like uncorked champagne. Or maybe that was nausea. Hard to tell.

She quickly finished transferring the patient to the bed, then helped Mario wheel their empty gurney out to the hallway.

"I need to get a drink," Isabella said. "Meet you back at the ambulance."

"*Sí.*" Mario took the gurney and headed out while Isabella made a beeline for the restrooms at the end of the hall, hot bile scalding her throat.

After she'd finished tossing her cookies, she splashed some cold water on her face, then stared at herself in the mirror. Man, she looked as rough as she felt. Dark circles under her eyes, cheeks a bit hollow from being unable to keep much down the past few days, her complexion tinged green. A far cry from the last time she'd seen Carlos on the beach.

That night seemed like a fantasy now. The dinner, the drinks, the conversation. After they'd finished at El Chiringuito, they'd strolled along the beach, laughing and talking and eventually holding hands. Then, under the stars, they'd kissed. The chemistry had been instant and hot as hell. She rarely let people close, rarely let herself be vulnerable and free and wild, but with Carlos, she had. Maybe it was the novelty of it, or the fact that they both knew it was just a one-off, an uncomplicated night of sex and fun, that had made her so reckless. Whatever it was, she'd dived in headfirst and reveled in it.

They'd gone back to her flat, since it was closer, and basically fallen on each other the minute they'd gotten through the door. Clothes came off and inhibitions vanished. She'd been unable to get enough of him, touching him, kissing him, tasting him everywhere. He'd done the same to her, bringing her to orgasm over and over with his lips and tongue and fingers before finally entering her. It had been a long time. Too long, and he'd filled her completely. And when he'd moved… Well, it felt like her entire universe had shifted. They'd both been desperate for each other, straining, reaching and finally capturing that brief, bright pinnacle of pleasure, exploding into a thousand shards of brilliant light before floating softly down into the shadows and falling asleep wrapped in each other's arms.

When Isabella had woken up the next day, Carlos was gone. He'd left behind a rose on her pillow and a scribbled note, saying "thanks for the memory."

She'd kept his stupid note, for some reason, stuffed in her nightstand drawer, thinking it would be her one memento of that night. But now…

Gripping the edge of the vanity counter tight, Isabella rode out another wave of nausea, thankfully not dry heaving this time, then finally took a deep breath. In and out. In and out. She hated being sick to her stomach worse than anything in the world, and luckily she hardly ever became ill. Well, until recently, anyway.

Once she felt marginally better, she washed her hands, then headed out. She could still use the drink she'd mentioned to Mario, so instead of heading toward the ambulance bay, she took the elevator down to the basement cafeteria instead. Time for a break about now anyway, and maybe tea and crackers would soothe her stomach.

"Blood pressure's up to one two six over eighty-two," Carlos said, checking the kid again in the trauma bay.

"All right," Dr. Gonçalo said in Spanish. "I'm going to take a look at your chest now, *sí*?"

The kid groaned in pain but nodded.

The doctor did a quick but thorough exam, talking throughout. "Large, deep contusions over the pectoral area and sternum, consistent with a blunt impact from the steering wheel. Fifth and sixth ribs on the left fractured. Breath sounds are normal, but I want to make sure there's no bruising or injuries to the lungs from the accident. Please order an X-ray and CT."

Carlos nodded and typed the orders into his tablet as Dr. Gonçalo gave them, doing his best to stay in the moment and not dwell on his shock at seeing Isabella again. He'd known she was a paramedic, so the chance existed, he supposed, with him being an ER nurse. But Barcelona was a large city, and he'd figured the chances of them running into each other again were slim.

From the startled look in her eyes and the way she'd raced out of here like her butt was on fire after transferring the patient, she'd felt much the same way.

Carlos finished typing, then waited until Dr. Gonçalo finished her exam before following her out of the trauma bay. "I'll get right on those orders, Doc. And I'll get ahold of his next of kin."

"Thanks," Dr. Gonçalo said before rushing off to her next case.

The elevators dinged, and Carlos looked up

in time to see Isabella get on, heading down to the basement, according to the green arrow above the doors.

Huh. His first instinct said go after her. But no. He had work to do. Besides, he wasn't here to get a girlfriend. He was here to work. Work and find out more about his father's family. The father who hadn't even cared enough about him to stick around after he'd gotten Carlos's mom pregnant.

Not that he was bitter or anything. Hell, he'd moved beyond bitter at ten years old.

Now, at thirty-four, he was more curious than anything.

Curious why a man would sire a child, with a woman he supposedly cared about deeply, then disappear without a trace. Granted, his father hadn't known about him at the time, but his mother and her parents had written to him repeatedly to tell him. Those letters had never been returned, so where did they go? The mystery persisted. What wasn't a mystery, however, was how Carlos had been treated, growing up a bastard in Cuba. Always on the lookout, always careful, knowing some kids would beat him up for his lineage, or lack thereof. Cuba might be a Communist country, but many people were old-school religious, and unwed girls and their babies were not exactly celebrated on their island. So, Carlos had developed a thick skin, learned to keep his emotions inside, to never show vulnerability to those who wanted to hurt him.

His old habit allowed him to keep things low-key now. Even in the high-pressure situations of the ER, Carlos never lost his cool. Getting angry or defensive only made things worse, in his opinion, so he strived to keep an even keel as much as possible.

But as he set up the CT scan and X-rays, his stubborn mind kept going back over his night with Isabella. The way she'd felt in his arms, the way she'd tasted of wine and wonderful abandon when he'd kissed her. The way she'd cried out his name like a prayer and a benediction all rolled into one when she'd come apart beneath him, around him…

"Here for the rib fractures," a tech said, stopping at the nurses' station, jarring Carlos out of his erotic thoughts.

He cleared his throat and frowned at his computer screen. "Trauma bay two."

Enough. Time to stop daydreaming about his one-night stand and start focusing on the patient under his care. He waited until the radiology techs wheeled the kid out of the ER and toward the elevators and the CT scanner, then made calls to the kid's family to let them know he was in the ER and okay. They were upset but thankful and said they'd be there shortly.

Done, he checked his watch, then stared down the hall toward the elevators. Time for his break, and it would be another hour or so before the CT and X-rays were done, given the busy radiology schedule. So, yeah. He'd grab a snack. And if he happened to run into Isabella, so be it. They should say something to each other, anyway, since they'd be working together. No sense making things more awkward than they already were, right? It would be fine. Great. Okay.

But as he boarded the elevator, his stomach fell for more reasons than just the ride.

That night had been special. A fantasy of sorts.

Am I ready to let the fantasy go and return to reality?

The night at the bar on the beach felt like a moment out of time. It had been so easy with her—talking, laughing. Easy to feel comfortable with her. For an expat from Cuba, still trying to get his bearings in a new city and a new country, it had been like balm to his soul. Made him feel less alone here, if only for a little while.

Not that he didn't have support. His uncle had been more than welcoming to him, even going so far as to rent the flat above his popular bar, Encanteri, to Carlos at a reduced rate. Cuba had much more affordable housing, so seeing a sixty-square-meter flat go for luxury prices had been a bit of a shock. His uncle Hugo had looked out for him, though. Said he felt responsible for Carlos after inviting him here to live, so, yeah. Plus, the place was clean and safe and fully furnished, so a guy couldn't argue, right?

He'd had many people over the years ask him why he chose nursing instead of continuing his education and becoming a doctor. He'd had the grades for it. But he hadn't wanted to spend more years in school. He'd wanted to get out and get to working with patients right away. And so he'd chosen nursing, because everyone who'd spent any time in a medical setting knew that the nurses had the real power, anyway. Doctors gave the orders, but the nurses were the ones on the front lines carrying them out.

The elevator dinged. The doors swished open and he stepped off, then held them for an elderly couple to board before heading down the hall for the cafeteria, the smells of baking cheese and fried food beckoning him. Unfortunately, though, he'd lost his appetite. Tension knotted his stomach, only getting worse when he spotted Isabella across the room, sitting in a secluded corner of the atrium.

He got himself an iced tea and paid at the register, flashing his employee badge for his discount. He shouldn't be nervous talking to her again. They were both adults. It would be fine. Besides, the night they'd met, they'd worked so well together on the heart attack victim. Been in sync from the first. No reason they couldn't continue now, eh? He thanked the cashier and picked up his tea to head to her table, and then she looked up and saw him, and nope.

Any hopes they could just pretend that night had never happened evaporated.

Something about the haunted, hunted look in her eyes made him pause.

Carlos took a deep breath, his chest aching, then slowly continued over to her table. The wariness in her expression only worsened the closer he got, and he wanted to tell her it would be okay. Wanted to tell her he wouldn't bring it up, it was already forgotten, even if it wasn't. Even if he'd never forget that night and the way she'd made him feel like more than an unwanted, abandoned kid whose father didn't care enough about him to make any contact at all. Who would never have a chance to talk to his father, to ask him why he'd run away, because his father had died ten years prior.

Shit.

Carlos shoved all that out of his mind. Until he'd come to Barcelona, he'd gotten on fine without thinking about his father. Of course, his mother's family never brought him up, either, which helped. For her part, his mother had been wonderful. Always loving and supportive and caring, as much a friend and confidante as a parent. They'd been as close as mother and son could be, because they only had each other. And while she'd never said anything specifically about how she'd felt being abandoned by the man she'd loved and lost, well...he could see it in her eyes, the permanent scars it had left on her soul. One more thing he didn't let past his barriers, that he kept hidden deep inside, because it hurt too much to bring it out into the light.

But then his mother had passed away last

year, and he'd been devastated. As the last surviving member of their little family, it had fallen on Carlos to go through her things. Then he'd found the name of his uncle Hugo, the first relative on his father's side Carlos had discovered. And, being a believer in fate, he'd seen it as a call to his destiny. The same call he'd felt with his immediate and intense attraction to Isabella on the beach in April.

Before he could say anything, though, she blinked up at him, gaze inscrutable. "What do you want?"

"I..." he started, then stopped.

I want to start over. I want to get back to the happy, easy, connection we had. I want to thank you for that night.

He settled for, "We need to talk."

CHAPTER TWO

ISABELLA FROZE LIKE a deer in headlights the minute she saw Carlos heading her way. Too late now, though, so she sat there, first studying her phone, then looking up at him with as impassive a gaze as she could manage. "What do you want?"

Ouch.

Cold. Far colder than she'd wanted, and way colder than she felt inside. Honestly, she was burning up, and it had nothing to do with her nausea earlier and everything to do with man standing before her. She hid her wince, though barely.

If he took offense at her tone, he didn't show it, just watched her with those dark eyes of his. The emotions flickering through them were fascinating—desire, embarrassment, pleasure, pain. "I..."

Her heart stuttered, then slammed against

her rib cage. What? What would he say? He regretted that night? It had been a mistake? Best forgotten? She'd certainly tried to put it out of her mind, but nope. Impossible. Those memories kept resurfacing. The two of them entwined in her sheets, entwined in each other, making love until the early morning hours, then parting ways.

"We need to talk," he said at last.

Yes. Talk. Good.

She swallowed hard, then glanced around. Too many other staff members were there. Too many nosy listeners. The gossip around St. Aelina's had just recently moved on from cardiothoracic surgeon Dr. Caitlin McKenzie falling for her temporary colleague, Dr. Javier Torres, after news got out he wasn't just a cardiothoracic surgeon like Cait, but an actual fabulously wealthy count. She'd met them a while ago when bringing in a patient with chest injuries from a car accident requiring their expertise. Isabella didn't want to be the next hot topic of conversation around here. So, she stood and gestured toward the exit. "Fine. But not here."

Carlos blinked at her a moment, then followed her out into the hall. There were several on-call rooms down here for the doctors to use to rest on long shifts, and Isabella found one empty for privacy. She flipped the sign and held the door for Carlos before closing it behind them.

"So..." she said, crossing her arms. Having a bed right there was more than a little awkward. They both glanced at it, then looked away fast. She cleared her throat and tried again, rushing ahead because maybe it would hurt less. Like ripping off a bandage. "Look, if this is about our..." Isabella made a vague gesture between them. "One night we had together, don't worry. I won't say anything. It's already forgotten."

Liar. No way she'd forget that night with him. Not possible.

His color drained a bit beneath his tan, and she felt bad again. She'd always been one to play her emotions close to her chest—less vulnerable that way—but he was nothing if not passionate. Both in and out of bed. Everything he felt was right there, just below the surface.

Sweat broke out on her forehead, and her stomach lurched. Oh, God. She was going to be sick again. Not here. Not now. Not in front of him. Too late. She turned to grab the counter but missed, stumbling forward and nearly falling on the floor. Feeling shaky and stupid, she allowed him to help her to sit on the edge of the bed. Carlos crouched beside her, taking her wrist to check her pulse.

"Hey, hey," he said, his voice soothing the roiling heat radiating off her cheeks. Through the haze of sudden dizziness, she held on to his hand like a lifeline, focusing on her breath. In, out. In, out. Until, finally, the nausea eased, and her vision cleared. Carlos still crouched beside her, holding her hand and stroking her hair back from her face. "You're okay. It's okay. Do you want to lie down?"

She shook her head, not trusting herself to speak yet.

"All right." He stood and dumped his tea in the sink, then rinsed the cup and filled it with water before returning to her side again. "Drink some of this if you can. It will help. When was the last time you ate?"

Isabella sipped, grateful for the coolness on her dry throat, washing away the sting of bile. "Uh, last night, I guess. I had a couple crackers this afternoon before work. I've had this stomach bug for a few days, so…"

"Okay." He took a deep breath, then straightened. "Well, it's probably not a bad idea for someone to take a look at you before you go back out on ambulance runs."

"Oh, no. I'm sure I'll be fine." She set the cup aside and tried to stand. Too fast, though, and her head spun again. She sank down on the bed and covered her face with her hands. Mario had to be wondering where she was by now. She needed to get back to work, but she just felt so icky.

Carlos snorted. "Fine people don't nearly collapse on the floor. Seriously. Let me help you upstairs to the ER. I'll have one of the doctors check you out. Maybe eat a cookie or two. I'm sure you'll be fine."

Isabella wanted to argue but couldn't. He was right. Maybe she should get checked out, get some meds or something and be done with it. She needed to be cleared anyway before going back out on runs with Mario. Standard policy.

"Okay." She got up again, this time with Carlos beside her, supporting her elbow. "Let's go, then." They started out, but she stopped with one foot into the hallway. "Are we okay with the other thing?"

Carlos's tanned cheeks flushed, and she found it far too endearing. "*Si.* We're okay."

"Good."

They rode the elevator back up to the first floor, and Carlos walked with her into the ER, then put her in an empty trauma bay. "Wait here," he said. "I'll grab one of the doctors. Be right back."

A few moments later, her friend Nina, a nurse, came in, smiling sympathetically. "Hi, Issy. What's wrong? Carlos said you're having some nausea, dizziness, too?"

"*Si.*" Isabella explained her symptoms and how long they'd been going on. "I'm pretty sure it's the flu or something. You know how those things go around."

"Yep. We've been seeing a lot of cases lately." Nina typed in some notes on the computer in the corner. "And when was your last period?"

"Oh…uh…" Isabella frowned. Come to think of it, it had been a while. But she'd never been exactly regular, and with all the stress she'd been under recently with work and all, not unusual for it to be late. She gave the last date to the nurse, then waited for her to complete her documentation.

"All right. Let me just run all this by the doctor and see what she wants to do," Nina said, smiling. "Hold tight."

Isabella waited a few more minutes for

her friend to return, this time with a specimen cup in hand and a phlebotomist in tow. "Okay." Nina handed her the cup. "We need a urine sample, and we're going to take some blood for a CBC and to make sure your blood sugar isn't low."

"Where's Carlos?" Isabella asked as the phlebotomist got to work.

"He had other patients," Nina said. "Do you want me to get him?"

"No, no. It's fine."

The fact she kind of wished he was still there with her made her even more determined not to ask for him now. She didn't like to depend on other people.

The phlebotomist finished, and Isabella used the restroom to leave her sample, then more waiting. She managed to flag down Mario and let him know what was going on. Luckily it was a slower shift, emergency-wise, and there was another unit on call as backup, so they weren't short-staffed. Mario even got her some juice and a granola bar from the vending machine down the way. She felt much better after eating.

Finally, the curtain around her trauma bay opened and a doctor stepped inside, sans Nina.

"Ms. Rivas?" the doctor said. It wasn't

someone she recognized, so probably new. Maybe a resident. "I'm Dr. De Leon. We've got your test results back."

"Is it the flu?" she asked, ready put this whole embarrassing situation behind her.

"No. Not the flu." The doctor smiled. "I'm happy to tell you, Ms. Rivas, that you're pregnant. Congratulations."

Time seemed to slow. Isabella shook her head, sure she'd misheard. "I'm sorry?"

"Nausea is extremely normal, especially during the first trimester." The doctor scrolled through the file on a tablet in their hand. "Based on the date of your last period, I'd say you're about eight weeks along. I'll have Nina get you set up with prenatal vitamins and the name of an OB here in Barcelona, unless you already have someone."

Oddly numb, Isabella just shook her head. Pregnant? That couldn't be possible. She didn't sleep around and was always careful and used protection. The last time she'd been with anyone…

Oh, God.

No. No, no, no. This could not be happening. She could not be pregnant with Carlos's baby, the guy she'd just brushed off and nearly fainted in front of. No. Just nope.

The doctor left, and Nina came back in, cringing slightly. "Oh, gosh, Issy. I'd say congratulations, but from the look on your face, I'm not sure if I should."

Dazed didn't begin to cover how Isabella felt about the news. But as the shock slowly wore off, cold fear set in. She couldn't be a mother. She'd already spent ten years raising her younger siblings after their mother died. Then their dad had fallen ill a few years later, and it had been her responsibility to care for him as well. Her siblings were now scattered all over Spain, leaving her behind to build a life for herself alone. Hell, the only one of her siblings she even spoke with on a regular basis was Diego, and only because he'd moved back here and worked at St. Aelina's.

Her stomach lurched again, but for very different reasons now.

"Oh, Issy," Nina said, walking over to rub her back. "I'm sorry. If there's anything I can do, any way I can help…"

"I'm fine." She slid off the table, her legs steady beneath her once more. Good thing, too, since the rest of her world had been totally rocked. "I'm a bit surprised. That's all." She opened the curtain to head out, not fine at all. The opposite, really, but she'd get through it like she always did—on her own. "I need to get back to work."

Work helped. Work would always help. Isabella hoped so, anyway.

A few hours later, Carlos waited by the ambulance bay doors for an incoming case. Seventeen-year-old male who'd gotten a deep wrist laceration while surfing. They'd called down one of the ortho guys to consult, a Dr. Manuel Pérez.

He was glad for the distraction to get his mind off the disastrous meeting with Isabella earlier. God, could he have handled that any worse? Images of her gray face, her wary eyes, flashed in his head. And when she'd almost passed out on him, his stress levels had skyrocketed. He'd gone back to the trauma bay to check on her after he'd finished with a couple of other patients, but Nina had said she'd already left.

Our one night we had together, don't worry. I won't say anything. It's already forgotten...

Her words kept looping in his mind, cutting deep each time.

Because Carlos hadn't forgotten. Not at all. And though he'd never ask for more from her if she wasn't interested, casual hookups weren't his thing. That night, however brief, had meant something to him. It had made him feel less alone in a new city, for one. Had made him feel like he'd made a real connection with her, for two. The fact she hadn't felt the same hurt. Understandable, but it stung.

Then the automatic doors swooshed open, and reality snapped back fast. The EMTs wheeled in their patient, the guy moaning and writhing in pain, a blood-soaked beach towel clutched to his right wrist as they headed for the next open trauma bay. Of course, it was Isabella and her partner who'd brought him in. Carlos's heart jumped into his throat again as he took position alongside the gurney, guiding it down the hall.

Dr. Pérez followed along beside Carlos. "What have we got?"

Isabella frowned, staring straight ahead as she gave the rundown. "This is Felipé. He's seventeen, heavy bleeding from a deep laceration to his right wrist while surfing. Says he cut it on some sharp rocks near the Killers. I've been there myself and can attest those rocks are dangerous."

"I see." Dr. Pérez followed them into trauma bay one, waited until they'd transferred the patient from the gurney to the hospital bed, then proceeded to remove the towel from the patient's wrist to better examine it. Carlos stood by with gauze to stanch the bleeding in case an artery had been hit. "Sir," Dr. Pérez said to the patient, "can you tell me, when the accident occurred, did the blood squirt or ooze?"

"I don't know," the patient said, eyes glassy with pain. "I just grabbed a towel to put on it as soon as I saw the blood."

"It's down to the bone," Dr. Pérez said, peering at the wound. He performed a quick exam before glancing over at Carlos. "What's his blood pressure?"

"One two six over eighty-four," Carlos said, watching as Isabella and her partner left the trauma bay. Damn. He'd hoped to talk to her again.

"Okay. Sir? Can you open your fingers the whole way?" Dr. Pérez asked, drawing Carlos's attention back to the patient. The boy did as the doctor asked. "Nice. Okay. Patient has pretty good motor function. Good pulse here, too. Looks like a venous bleed that just went through the muscle to me. Tendons appear pretty much intact."

Carlos smiled at the patient. "That's good news."

The patient nodded then swallowed hard.

"Right." Dr. Pérez stepped back as another nurse applied pressure to the wound while Carlos checked the monitors hooked up to the patient. "From what I can see now, Felipé, the cut went through the muscle, but it appears your tendons are okay. The major stuff is intact, all right?"

Felipé nodded again, cringing in pain.

"I'm going to order some tests for you, make sure there's nothing more serious going on there I've missed." Dr. Pérez turned to Carlos again as other staff members flocked around the patient, attaching an IV and a O2 sat monitor to the guy's finger. "Let's get a stat MRI and X-rays of that wrist. Then book an OR suite upstairs so I can get that laceration repaired."

"*Si*, Doctor." Carlos followed him out of the room and back to the nurses' station. "I'll have them page you once the results are in."

They hadn't had a chance to even register the kid yet, but it didn't matter. St. Aelina's was a teaching hospital and took a lot of cases other facilities turned away. Part of the reason he'd taken the job here. He'd expected to be busy and hadn't been disappointed so far. Busy was good. Kept him from dwelling on the other reason he was in Barcelona—to find out more about the father who'd walked out on him and his mother before Carlos had even been born.

Once he'd gotten the patient scheduled for his MRI and the techs came to wheel the patient away, Carlos took a much-deserved break. He'd been on duty in the ER for hours already and had another seven hours ahead of him before his shift was done. Time outside would do him good. He left word with the charge nurse he was going on break, then headed toward the ambulance bay. He had his phone with him in case they had to call him back in sooner than the hour he'd clocked out for.

After stepping through the automatic doors, Carlos took a deep breath and stared up into the starry sky. Closer now to midnight than dusk. The quiet chirp of crickets filled the cool night air and helped release some of his stress.

"Hey." The soft greeting made him jump. He'd thought he was alone out here. Carlos looked over to see Isabella leaning against the wall, her ambulance parked and ready a short way away.

His pulse tripped and blood pounded. Just like that, he was back in that on-call room downstairs, feeling like a bumbling idiot with the woman he couldn't get out of his mind, even all this time later. She looked better now, her cheeks pink and her eyes sparkling. Still wary, but brighter.

She sighed and rested her head back against the cool stone of the building and looked at him. "Maybe we can have that talk now?"

"Uh, sure." He ran his palms down the front of his green scrub pants, then walked over to lean against the wall beside her, remembering her caution earlier. "Here, or..."

"Can we walk a bit?" she asked, then called down to her partner, "I'll be right back. Text me if another call comes in."

Mario waved back from inside the rig.

"How about the beach?" Isabella asked as they walked up the ramp to the street level. "It's not far from here. Just a block or so."

"Uh, sure." They strolled along, both quiet, until Carlos asked. "Are you feeling better?"

"Yes, thanks."

Right. She still hadn't really looked at him since they'd locked eyes over the bed back in the trauma bay. He wasn't sure exactly what would happen or what she would say after basically telling him she'd forgotten all about him and their night together, but his instincts said this was important, so he stayed and didn't try to push it or rush her. Whatever she had to say, she'd tell him in her own good time. Carlos had learned over the years to be patient.

They reached the boardwalk in front of Playa de Bogatell and walked for a while, the sound of the waves crashing onshore mixing with the conversations of tourists and the caws of seagulls. Scents of sand and food from the bars nearby drifted on the air, and a couple of cyclists whizzed past, making him move closer to Isabella, excusing himself.

Finally, they stopped near a deserted section of railing. A slight breeze ruffled their hair as they both looked out at the sea, blowing some stray strands from the low ponytail at the base of her neck against her cheeks. From somewhere, a low, sweet ballad played, suiting the oddly poignant feel of the moment.

Isabella inhaled deep, then mumbled something he didn't quite catch, still not looking at him.

"*Perdóneme?*" *Excuse me?* She couldn't have said what he thought she'd said, because that would mean…

She sighed, then turned to face him. "I'm pregnant."

Carlos blinked at her for a beat or two, thinking he must have misheard, but nope. She'd said it. *Pregnant.* His brain swirled with a thousand different thoughts at once, short-circuiting his vocal cords. *A baby. She's having a baby. My baby. I'm having a baby.* Those ideas quickly ricocheted to the opposite extreme. *I'm not ready to be a father. How will I raise a child? We were careful that night. We used protection.* Except, now that he remembered back to that evening with Isabella, they'd both had a lot to drink, and things were a bit…murky once they'd hit her bedroom, so… Oh, God. His pulse raced and sweat prickled the back of his neck, making him shiver slightly in the cool night breeze off the ocean. *Say something. Anything.*

He managed to croak out, "*Qué?*" *What? Not helpful, dude.*

"I'm pregnant," she repeated, not looking overjoyed about it. "And it's yours."

"Oh," he said, the words finally starting to sink in past his shock, a weird sense of pure joy and fierce protectiveness swarming his system all at once. They were having a baby. *My baby. My child.* And while he appreciated her clarifying for him, it wasn't necessary. He'd believed her the first time. *Father. I'm going to be a father. Please, God, let me do better than my own* padre *did for me.*

He vowed to himself then and there he would. Whatever it took.

Then her lack of enthusiasm landed hard, along with the fear in her eyes, though she tried to hide it. His heart sank. Perhaps she would not keep it. Carlos rested an elbow on the railing, knowing he needed to say something but also wanting to tread carefully. She needed reassurance. They both did. And the last thing he wanted was for this to go south again, like before. He cleared his throat around the lump of uncertainty there and hoped he sounded more sure than he felt at the moment. "Okay. Well, please know that I'll be there for you however you need me to be. Okay?"

CHAPTER THREE

At first, Isabella wasn't sure how to respond. She'd expected him to be shocked, surprised, maybe even a little defiant about the fact that she'd said the baby was his. After all, they really didn't know each other well. One night of sex didn't make a relationship, no matter how glorious.

The fact he'd just stepped right up and offered to help, though… Well, that knocked her back a step, frankly. Growing up the oldest of her siblings, she was used to people passing the buck of responsibility on to the next person. And the next person. And the next person. Until, usually, it ended up in Isabella's lap to deal with. She'd come to expect it, really, so having Carlos be right there with his offer of aid took a bit of getting used to. On the heels of that came another revelation—one that she wasn't sure made her as happy. If he'd offered to help, that meant he wasn't going anywhere.

While she tried to formulate her answer, he added, "How about we go have a drink and talk? My treat."

"Oh, uh..." She scrambled for an excuse. Not because she didn't want to spend more time with him, but because she did. And relying on people got into dangerous territory for her. "Don't you have to return to work?"

Carlos checked his smart watch. "Not for another twenty minutes. Come on," he said, gesturing for her to follow him back toward the hospital. "I know a place not far from here."

She hesitated, glancing over at El Chiringuito, the bar they'd gone to that first night. "What about there?"

He gave a dismissive wave. "Nah. I think you'll like this place better. Trust me." The tiredness and nausea from earlier still lurked around her edges, with the shocking news she'd received and, well, everything. Plus, she was thirsty again, so... "Fine."

They headed back toward the hospital, but instead of taking a left toward St. Aelina's, they went right, down a block and a half, then stopped before a gray stone building on the corner. The large blocks were rough-hewn, giving the place an old-world feel. Barcelona was known for its beautiful and artistic architecture, and this place fit right in. From the arched windows to the flower boxes overflowing with roses, it had a medieval feel to it. Fancy, too. An intricate, hand-painted sign above the door proclaimed the bar's name—Encanteri.

"Uh…maybe we should go somewhere else," Isabella said, balking at the entrance. She still wore her EMT uniform, and Carlos wore his scrubs. "I don't think I'm dressed for this place."

"Nonsense," he said, opening the door and holding it for her. His grin made her gut tingle for completely different reasons now. He was gorgeous. No doubt about it. He winked, and her heart fluttered. "This is my uncle's bar. Remember? I told you he owned it the first night. It's fine."

"Oh, I…" Isabella said as he put his hand at the small of her back. The heat of his touch penetrated the cotton of her shirt and made her far more aware of him than was wise. Although this place looked much fancier than what she'd expected, and she really wasn't dressed for this, he ushered her through the door anyway.

Inside, the bar lived up to its namesake of a magical spell or charm—two stories high, with lots of jars filled with what looked like bubbling potions and walls lined with glass canisters filled with brightly colored liquids. Near the center of the bar sat a contraption that appeared to come straight from a laboratory, with tubes and wires and fizzing concoctions flowing through it. The dark wood bar stretched along one side of the place, and small tables for two or four filled the other half. A balcony ran around the upper story where people stood and mingled, drinks in hand. She'd heard of this place before but had never been inside.

"You really know the owner?" she asked Carlos, voice barely above a whisper.

"I do." He gave her a side glance and another grin, then raised his hand in greeting to a stout older man behind the bar with short, thick gray hair. "That's my uncle Hugo, owner of Encanteri."

"Uh...okay. Wow." Isabella followed him up to the bar, where he introduced her. "Uncle Hugo, please meet Isabella Rivas. We're..."

Carlos looked back at her then to his uncle again. "Friends."

"*Hola*, Isabella Rivas," the older man said, shaking her hand firmly. "Hugo Sanchez. Welcome to my bar."

"Thank you." She matched Hugo's friendly smile, noticing his accent—the same as Carlos's. "The place is lovely. Are you also from Cuba originally?"

"*Sí.*" Hugo smiled and patted his nephew on the arm. "I've been in Barcelona for nearly forty years now, but Havana will always be home. Finally convinced this one to come see me, too."

Carlos chuckled. "*Sí.* You did. Can we get a couple of sparkling waters, please, Uncle? We'll get a table in the corner there."

"Of course." Hugo waved to Isabella, then turned to get their drinks while they walked across the narrow room to a table for two in a secluded corner. Carlos held her chair for her and took a seat across the tiny table from her. Their knees kept brushing under the table, much the same as the first night they'd met, conjuring more memories for her.

"So," Isabella said, after the server who brought their drinks left. "You moved here to be closer to your uncle?"

"*Si.*" He flashed her a sad smile. "And to find out more about my biological father."

"Oh?" she said, glad for a topic to discuss that didn't involve her or the pregnancy she hadn't quite come to terms with yet. They would have to discuss it at some point, but maybe not tonight. "Was he from Barcelona?"

"No." Carlos's smile faded to a frown. "Well, honestly, I don't know much about him. He left my mother before she had me. After she passed away last year, I found Uncle Hugo's name in some of my mother's paperwork and decided to go exploring." He shrugged. "Only after I moved here did I find out my father passed away ten years ago."

"I'm so sorry." Isabella reached for his hand without thinking, then pulled away fast.

"Thank you." He sipped his water. "Anyway, from what I've been able to piece together from Uncle Hugo, Alejandro—my father—was from Cuba originally, but his family traveled a lot back and forth from Havana to Barcelona. In fact, he and my mother met here in Barcelona over a holiday. They had a whirlwind romance, and she ended up pregnant with me. Unfortunately, she didn't realize it until she returned to Cuba again with her parents. They were very upset and tried to contact my father and his family but couldn't get ahold of them. They never heard from him again, actually."

"Yikes. That's awful."

"Hmm." He sat back in his chair, stretching out his long legs in front of him and causing those scrubs of his to stretch over his muscled body most enticingly. Not that she noticed. Nope. "Sounds silly, but I brought my mother's diary with me. Thought maybe I could retrace their steps here in Barcelona, visit some of the same romantic spots they did, to try and discover more about him and who they were together."

Intrigued despite herself, Isabella leaned closer, resting her arms atop the table. "That sound so cool. And interesting, too. I'd love to see that diary sometime."

"How about now?" Carlos asked, surprising her.

"Oh, uh..." Isabella sat back, unsure.

Some of her uncertainty must've shown on her face, because Carlos laughed and patted her arm. "I live above this place. It will take like two seconds for us to run up there, and I can show it to you." His smile faltered. "I mean, unless you don't feel comfortable doing that with me. I wouldn't want to pressure you into—"

"No. It's fine," she said quickly. Better than focusing on her and the pregnancy when she still had no idea what to do about that yet. She checked her watch. "I can give you five minutes, then I need to get back to Mario and the rig."

"Let's go!" Carlos stood and waved to his uncle, then led Isabella back outside and to a small set of wrought iron stairs behind the building. They led to a third-floor flat considered luxurious and premium by Barcelona standards. Two-bedrooms, one-bath, a full kitchen with laundry facilities, large living room–dining area, and even a small balcony in the back. "My uncle gives me a break on the rent here, otherwise I'd never be able to afford it on my nurse's salary. Have a seat and I'll get the diary."

She did as he asked, taking a spot on the end of the overstuffed white sofa. Her own place was about the same size, maybe a little bigger, with an extra small bedroom she used as a home office. The view here at Carlos's was much better, though. He could see the beach from his balcony, while hers beheld a sea of more rooftops.

He returned a moment later with the diary and handed it to her. "There's a bookmark there where the story of their holiday together begins."

Isabella opened to it and began to read. Most of the places mentioned she'd been to many times, having lived in the city her whole life. La Sagrada Familia. Park Güell. Casa Milà. The usual tourist spots. Places his mother, Ana, would've visited with her parents, most likely. But a few were more romantic—Passeig de Gracia at night, El Borne with its exclusive boutiques, the gorgeous roses at the Rosalada de Cervantes and the garden maze at El Labyrinth d'Horta. Those, she imagined, would be perfect getaways for a young couple in love. Before she could think better of it, she said, "I know these places well. I'd be happy to show you around if you like."

Why did I say that?

Her plan had been to tell him about the pregnancy, then back away slowly, get some space between them again until she figured out her end of things. Now, she'd basically committed herself to being his tour guide. That would involve lots of time together, which meant lots of talking, which meant opening up and sharing things, and—ugh.

Too late now, though, based on his radiant grin. "That would be wonderful! Thanks so much for offering. I'd really like that. A tour from a native. Plus, it will give us a chance to get to know more about each other."

Not if I can help it.

"Great." Isabella stood and pulled her phone out, staring at the blank screen. "Looks like another call has come in, per Mario. I need to get back."

"Sure, sure," he said, putting the diary on a shelf nearby then joining her at the door to follow her out, locking up behind them. "Me, too. I've still got the rest of my shift to finish." They went back down the stairs and headed toward St. Aelina's. Didn't say much until they were standing outside the ER again, and Carlos turned toward her. "Thank you again, Isabella. For offering to show me around. It means a lot. And I meant what I said earlier. Whatever you need, let me know and I'm there, okay? You're not alone in this, no matter what you decide."

She nodded and smiled, then waved before walking back to the rig.

You're not alone in this...

That's what scared her. Alone meant comfort. Alone meant security.

Alone never let you down or disappointed you.

Alone never left you behind.

CHAPTER FOUR

A WEEK LATER, Carlos stood in front of La Sagrada Familia—the large, unfinished minor Roman Catholic basilica in the Exiample district of the city—waiting for Isabella to show up to be his tour guide. According to his mother's diary, this was the first place she and his father had visited. After that night at his flat, he and Isabella had agreed to do their tour today, one of the few times they both had off work, and the weather was sunny and warm without being too hot. Perfect for walking, though he did worry about her overexerting herself with the pregnancy. Not that he'd tell her.

Things around the pregnancy were still a bit awkward. They'd talked more about it after that night, mainly in passing, when her team would bring in a patient for Carlos and the other ER staff to treat. They'd shared coffees in the cafeteria, or tea, in Isabella's case, and talked about tests she'd had done, due dates and so on, though Isabella still kept the situation a secret from everyone else. He wasn't sure why, exactly, except perhaps she was still deciding whether or not to keep the baby, or maybe because it was still early and things could go wrong. Either way, it left him on pins and needles, and he hadn't been sleeping well.

He took a seat on a shady bench nearby to wait, taking in the mishmash of languages around him. Back in Cuba, you mainly heard Cubano, with a smattering of Spanish and a bit of English. Here the main language with the locals was Catalan—just different enough for him to have difficulty picking it up at first, and he'd made many mistakes in talking with patients in the ER those first few weeks. But better that than not trying at all, because if there was one thing he'd noticed here, it was that the locals of Barcelona were fiercely loyal to their Catalan, with regular Spanish second and English third. Isabella had taken pity on him that first night, though, and they'd bonded over English and had stuck with it since. He appreciated that about her. Appreciated a lot of things.

Like how she'd given up her first free day in forever to show him around. He'd looked forward to it, probably far more than he should. But Carlos hoped that, being away from the hospital and their work, they could dive deeper, really get to know each other better and maybe—finally—he could discover where she stood on their baby.

Wasn't long before he spotted Isabella heading toward him across the crowded street. She wore a yellow sundress, which set off her tanned, toned body and long dark hair to perfection. She was gorgeous, no two ways about it, with her wide, friendly smile and legs for miles. Even now, if he closed his eyes, he could still remember the feel of those legs wrapped around him as he'd lost himself inside her, warm and wet and wonderful and…

"*Hola*," Isabella said, putting a hand atop her floppy sun hat to prevent it flying off in a strong breeze that gusted by. "Are you ready to go?"

"*Si*." Carlos stood and cleared his throat from the sudden constriction those steamy memories had caused. "Ready when you are."

As they stood in line to enter, Carlos looked up at the intricate carvings on the walls of the building, then farther up toward the three towers above them—the Jesus Christ tower, the Virgin Mary tower and the evangelist tower. Even with the cranes and scaffolding around them due to repairs and restorations, the place was magnificent. The Art Nouveau period had always been his favorite. He'd had several street artist friends back in Cuba who'd adopted that style in their work. So, to see the work of Antoni Gaudí, one of the masters of that type of architecture, up close and personal like this was amazing. He could see why his parents might have started to fall in love there.

Isabella must've noticed him staring upward, because she pointed to one of the towers. "Did you know that once the construction is completed, the Jesus Christ tower will be the tallest thing in Barcelona?"

"*Sí.*" He grinned at her. "I did know that. I did my homework for today."

"Really?" She gave him an appraising look. "Well, then you know that the cathedral itself was never finished during Gaudí's lifetime."

"*Sí,*" he said again. "But he did leave behind detailed drawings and blueprints, so they are able to continue work on the building now."

She looked impressed. "True. They're going to make it so people can go all the way up to the top of the Jesus tower once it's done. You'll be able to look out over the entire city and feel closer to God, as Gaudí intended originally."

Finally, after a few more minutes, their group went inside. First past the gorgeous Nativity doors with their lush green leaves and tiny pink birds, and then into the interior of the building. There, a hush fell over the world. Even though there were about twenty people in their group, you could hear a pin drop. The temperature dropped about ten degrees as the bright sunshine outside dimmed. Cool white stone surrounded them as they passed through the narthex and then into what Carlos could only describe as heaven on earth. Soaring ceilings, gilded arches and a rainbow prism of colors streaming through the gorgeous stained-glass windows. Columns that split like tree branches above to support the weight of the ceiling. All the intricate swirling lines and nature-themed carvings showed the beauty of creation and took his breath away. Isabella must've felt the same, because she moved closer to him, their hands brushing as they took in the glory around them.

"This is one of my favorite places in the city," she whispered reverently. "Growing up, I'd come here sometimes, just to sit and wonder about everything. After my mother died and my father got sick, it was my sanctuary."

His gaze flicked from the architecture around them to her face, her expression full of rapt awe. She looked even more beautiful now, if that was possible, and his heart squeezed. "I'm sorry about your mother. And your father."

Isabella looked at him, blinking for a second like it took her that moment to register what he said. Then her cheeks flushed pink, and her gaze darted away again. "Thank you."

He wished she'd let him in, reveal more about herself, but they had the whole day in front of them.

"And here," their group's guide said, "we are now in the central nave. The light in this case is defined by the color of the stained glass. At the east side, when the sun rises, there are the green and blue colors, because it's the Nativity facade. And it's turning the colors to the red, orange, yellow and a little bit dark at the Passion facade at the west, when the sun sets, so the experience and atmosphere will be different, depending on the time you come inside."

They spent a few more moments being dazzled by the glorious cathedral, then went back outside to continue their tour. Carlos wasn't sure how anything could be better than that, but being with Isabella, he was willing to be surprised.

"Should we visit Casa Milà next, since that's spot number two on the list? It was also designed by Gaudí, so it is somewhat related architecturally, too," Isabella asked as they moved back into the sunshine, the heat welcome after the cooler church.

"Of course." Carlos smiled and gestured for her to lead the way, and they started walking toward their next destination. Lots of people were out and about now, and the city seemed alive and sparkling. After the intimate feel of the cathedral tour, he was eager to keep the lines of communication open. "We don't really have anything like La Sagrada Familia in Cuba, but we do have our Museo de la Revolución." He raised his fist in the age-old sign of rebellion and defiance, then chuckled. "It's not nearly as grand as your cathedral, even though it's housed in the old presidential palace."

"Hmm." Isabella smiled, glancing sideways at him. "I've never been to Cuba. I've heard the beaches are good, though, even if it's illegal to surf there."

"True." Carlos chuckled. "There's actually a whole underground around it now. Young people who've watched a bunch of surf movies and thought they could do it, too. It's still a risk, though. For decades, all water activities were prohibited, including surfing, because they feared people were fleeing to America. Of course, people still went into the water and even did some surfing, but only in certain areas, and then the surfers had to make their own boards and things. It's quite a thing."

"Sounds like." They waited at a light to cross the street. "I wouldn't have done well there, growing up. Not sure what I would've done without my beach breaks. Surfing kept me sane during those years after losing my mom."

He waited until they were walking again to gently probe for more information, offering a bit more about himself, too. "My mother passed away last year, as I said. She had cancer. Ovarian. Stage four by the time they diagnosed it. Cuba has amazing medical facilities, but even they couldn't save her." He sighed, the old grief pinching his chest even now. "I still miss her. You?"

Isabella didn't answer right away, and he began to wonder if she would at all. But then, finally, she took a deep breath and said, "I miss my mother, too. She died of cancer, too, but brain. She had headaches and they got progressively worse. They discovered the tumor on a scan, and because of the type, fast-growing and inoperable, she died seven months later."

Her tone sounded so forlorn, he couldn't help reaching over and taking her hand in a show of support. She didn't pull away.

"We were all in shock. My youngest siblings were just babies then, too young to even know what happened. The older ones were sad and knew she died, but we had to keep going. As the oldest, I took over what I could, to help Papì. Then he got sick, too. Multiple sclerosis." She shrugged. "It's rarer in men, and from what I later found out, probably ran in his family, but yeah. By the time they diagnosed him, his symptoms were getting severe. The following year, he wasn't able to work anymore, and so I got a part-time job after school to help supplement the family's income."

"Oh, Isabella." He gave her fingers a reassuring squeeze. "I can't imagine how difficult that must've been for you."

She nodded, staring straight ahead, her eyes hidden now by large dark sunglasses, though he could feel the tension in her through their joined hands. "Hard, yes. But I survived it. It made me stronger, I think."

He'd always had a thing for strong women, having been raised by one himself. Which explained his ever-growing attraction to Isabella. Not just her beauty, but the person inside as he learned more about her. "Is that why you became a paramedic?" he asked. "Because of what happened to your mother and also your father's illness?"

"Maybe." Her expression turned thoughtful. "Probably the caretaker aspect, too. I'm used to taking care of other people, and I'm good at it."

Hmm. She was good at taking care of people, from what Carlos had seen so far, but he wanted to ask…

Who takes care of you?

Isabella had tried to keep the focus on the city that she loved that morning and not get too personal with him. A defense mechanism she used a lot, especially with her patients. Working with people during the worst times of their life, which health crises often were, tended to make patients feel closer to their caregivers than they normally would. They often told her things they never would otherwise. She once had a man rattle off his bank account numbers to her on the way to the hospital for a heart attack. He'd feared he wouldn't make it and wanted someone to know how to pay for his final expenses, if necessary. Other people told her secrets about their love lives or their children or their pasts. Emergencies bred intimacies. Or so it seemed.

But today wasn't an emergency. In fact, up until now, it had seemed relaxed and easy. Then he'd gone and asked about her family and those old wounds opened right back up again, stealing her oxygen.

Silly, really. She knew that. She was grown adult woman with a successful career and a life she loved. She shouldn't be hung up on the past anymore, shouldn't care about the sacrifices she'd made for her siblings so they could go off and leave her behind. Bitter bile burned hot in her throat before she swallowed it down. She didn't resent it. She didn't. She wasn't that kind of person.

Still difficult, though, remembering those years when she'd felt alone and exhausted and like everything was closing in on her.

She took a deep breath, raising her face to the bright sunshine, staring at the gorgeous pink pastel building in front of them. Man, she loved Barcelona. It was fun seeing it through new eyes with Carlos, too, even if she had no intention of telling him about her innermost feelings and hurts. Still, when she glanced over at him, those deep, dark eyes of his compelled her to share something with him, especially after he'd shared with her about his family.

Isabella sighed and went with the least painful thing she could find. "I became a paramedic because I wanted to help people, like you. But I also wanted the freedom of new experiences every day. New cases, new patients. I like not being tied down to the same place with the same people all the time."

"Hmm," he said as they stopped for another light, seemingly really considering her answer. Weighing it. She couldn't help noticing he still had a hold of her hand and hated to admit how nice it felt. She should've pulled away but couldn't bring herself to. Didn't want to think too hard about why. "Will you continue working after the baby's born?"

"I'll have to," she said, smiling at him before taking off across the street to the front of the Casa Milà once the light turned green, towing him along behind her. "Got to support myself, right?" He opened his mouth like he wanted to say more, but she didn't want to hear it. Couldn't hear it, in case he offered to take care of her and the baby. No. She had to keep her freedom. "Looks like the lines aren't too long to get inside. Let's get our tickets, eh?"

They headed off across the plaza toward the ticket booth, only to stop sharply at the sound of a woman screaming. "Help me! Help! My husband collapsed!"

Just like on the beach that first night, Isabella and Carlos switched immediately into medical mode. They sprinted over to where a middle-aged man in shorts and a Hawaiian shirt sprawled on the pavement, looking pale and lifeless.

"What happened?" Isabella asked, taking off her sun hat and setting it beneath her tote bag so it didn't blow away. "I'm a paramedic. Whatever you can tell me will be helpful."

"We're here from Texas. Out sightseeing. I told Henry to take it easy because it's so hot out, but he wouldn't listen. Just kept pressing on, saying we had to stay on schedule if we wanted to fit everything in this trip."

"Pulse and breathing are rapid," Carlos said, scowling as he met Isabella's eyes. "Skin hot and dry to the touch."

"Heatstroke," they said in unison.

"Right." Isabella looked up at the frantic woman again. "Ma'am, I need you to call 061. That's the emergency number here. They'll send help. Your husband needs to go to a hospital right away."

The woman turned away to do so while Isabella and Carlos focused on their patient.

"We need to get him into the shade," Carlos said, waving over a young guy nearby and speaking to him in rapid Spanish. "Can you grab his feet while I lift his shoulders? We'll carry him to the shade by the door there."

Together they lifted the patient and moved him while Isabella ran alongside them. "I could've helped you."

"No," Carlos said, his gaze flicking from her eyes to her abdomen then back again. "You couldn't."

She'd forgotten about the baby. What if she forgot when it really mattered?

Oh, God. She'd be a horrible mother. What the hell ever made her think she could do this?

Then, just as quickly as she fell into her funk, she climbed out of it. Focusing on her work, her patient. She'd deal with the pregnancy like she dealt with everything else in her life, because she didn't have a choice.

"Get his shirt open," Isabella said as they waited for the ambulance crew to arrive. "See if we can get some water to help cool him down."

The man's eyes fluttered open, and he tried to talk, but his words were slurred and slow.

"Please, sir, lay still," Isabella said, taking the bottle of water Carlos handed her and opening it to pour on the man's chest. It would soak his shirt, but better that than the alternative. "You're suffering from heatstroke. Just stay calm. We've got help on the way."

Carlos stood and surveyed the area. "I can hear the sirens. They're getting closer."

"Good." Isabella smiled down at her patient. "They'll be here in no time, and then we'll get you and your wife to the hospital."

She continued to fan the man with a souvenir booklet someone had handed her while a small crowd gathered around them, people snapping photos and taking videos of the scene. Isabella ignored all that, focused on keeping her patient comfortable while Carlos performed crowd control, then took over fanning duties for her when her wrist got tired. Again, they worked great together, not even needing to talk sometimes—just a look or gesture communicated what they needed.

Finally, the EMTs arrived, a different crew than Isabella usually worked with, since they were in a different section of the city now, but still efficient. They took over care of the patient and got him and his wife loaded into the rig.

The woman reached out and took Isabella's and Carlos's hands before they closed the doors on her. "Thank you both for your help. Not sure what we would've done without you."

"You're welcome," Carlos said.

"They're taking you to St. Aelina's hospital. Newest and best in the city," Isabella said, squeezing the woman's hand. "You'll be fine."

"Thank you," the woman said again, then

the EMTs closed the back doors to the ambulance and they were off.

For several seconds afterward, they both just stared after it, a bit stunned.

"Well, that was unexpected," Carlos said.

"Yeah." Isabella bent and picked up her tote and put her hat back on. "Seems we can't get away from work, even on our days off." She looked at the line, then back to Carlos. "Should we get our tickets now? Unless you'd rather not continue the tour."

"Are you kidding?" He laughed, a low, rich sound that made Isabella's knees wobble against her will. "There's nothing I'd love more than to spend the rest of the day with you. You were amazing there, by the way."

"Same," she said, smiling, realizing that she did feel the same way. Which both amazed and terrified her. Somehow, without even trying, he'd found a way past her barriers. Now she couldn't imagine anyone she'd want to spend her time with more than Carlos. "Let's get our tickets, then."

For some reason, his compliment made her feel warmer inside, and that heat had nothing to do with the temperatures outside. When they got up to the ticket counter, the man there refused to sell them anything. On the house, he said, for what they'd done to help the tourist. Isabella thanked him, then walked over to get in line again with Carlos. Once again, they moved to the head of the line, the other waiting people applauding them and thanking them for helping. Isabella couldn't help but smile. Nice to have your hard work recognized, even if she wasn't used to it.

Once inside, they followed a tour guide, who explained the history and architecture of the place much better than Isabella ever could.

"Welcome to Casa Milà, also known as La Pedrera or the Quarry in English. This structure is regarded as Antoni Gaudí's most iconic work of civic architecture due to its constructional and functional innovations, as well as its ornamental and decorative solutions, which broke with the architectural styles of his era." The tour guide waited as her assistant translated that into French, Spanish and Japanese for the tourists before continuing. "For Gaudí, La Pedrera represented the most advanced approach to a building on a chamfered street corner in the Eixample district of Barcelona. It consists of two blocks of flats, each with its own entrance, structured around two large, interconnected courtyards with ramps down to the garage for vehicles."

As they learned about the building's façade and curtain wall, the ornate wrought iron gates, and the fact that Gaudí had designed with an eye for the future, with a parking garage in the basement—even if only for carriages and not cars—Isabella became more aware of Carlos beside her than she'd expected. His gentle warmth, the solid, supportive feel of his body next to hers, the fact that working with him and seeing how cool and confident and competent he was under pressure, made him sexy as hell. At least to her.

Stop it.

"Hey," Carlos said, leaning in to whisper in her ear and making her shiver. "How about we skip the rest of this tour and head straight to the roof? While this is lovely, I could use some fresh air."

She nodded, and they slowly made their way to the back of the group before following the signs up to the roof. The building really was spectacular, with its colorful murals and gorgeous inner courtyard. But nothing beat the views from the top. They emerged onto the roof amid a sea of statues and walkways.

Other tourists milled about, but it wasn't nearly as crowded as below, and they found a spot near the railing overlooking the city with a nice breeze blowing around them.

"So, your parents got to know each other while touring Barcelona," Isabella said. "It's very romantic."

"It is." Carlos leaned his forearms on the railing beside her, his smiled relaxed as he looked her way. "Are you seeing anyone?"

A bit shocked, she shook her head. "Uh, no. I don't really have time for that right now. With work and everything. Besides, I'm young and enjoying my freedom."

"Hmm." Carlos tilted his head, his expression turning serious as his gaze flicked down to her abdomen, then back again. "That may change, though, yes?"

Frowning, she looked out at the cityscape again. Guilt squeezed her chest tight. She shouldn't worry about losing her freedom when the baby came. It was natural to have your life change after a birth. And she didn't feel guilty, really. More…scared.

A lump of pain lodged in her throat. She wouldn't be alone in this. Carlos had already pledged to help her in any way he could. He would be a good father, she could already tell. Generous, attentive, good-hearted. *But is being good enough?* The pinch in her heart grew stronger. Her own father had been such a good man. The best man, really. And still, he'd failed. Felled first by the loss of their mother and then later by a disease that no one saw coming. So, being good wasn't enough, but it would have to do. Because the only thing worse, in Isabella's opinion, than having a father not able to be there for their child, because of health or other reasons, would be for their baby to grow up with no father at all. As poor Carlos had done. And he still searched for the remnants of the man, even all these years later.

She didn't want that for her child. And while losing your parents was inevitable, no sense putting a child through that before their time. She should know.

Isabella felt Carlos's gaze on her and shrugged. "No. Not necessarily. Women raise children on their own and have careers all the time. Regardless, I will make it work. We will make it work."

"It's not easy, though."

"No. I imagine it's not." She sighed, resting her hip against the cool wrought iron. "Did your mother have a hard time raising you?"

He shrugged, turning away again. "She did okay. Her parents helped a lot, watching me while she worked and after school. Do you have people to help? You mentioned siblings."

"Sure," she said, though wasn't entirely convinced they'd run to her rescue. The youngest four—Eduardo, Frida, Luis and Paola—were scattered all over Spain now. Only Diego lived here, and he was busy with his new wife, Grace, so…

She and the baby would be fine on their own. Without thinking, she placed her hand over her abdomen. Until that moment, she hadn't realized she'd decided to keep it, but she had. She wanted this baby. More than she'd ever wanted anything else. With or without a partner to help raise it.

"That didn't sound too convincing," he said.

"No, I mean, I'll be fine. We'll be fine."

"You're keeping it, then?" he asked, the look on his face a mix of hope and hesitation that made her heart ache. "Our baby?"

"*Sí,*" she said, confirming it for herself and the world. "I'm keeping it."

Carlos grinned then, so brightly it rivaled the sun above, and it felt like a weight lifted off her chest. Before she could react, he leaned in and kissed her fast, then hugged her, enveloping her in his warmth and the scents of spices and soap and something indefinably Carlos. She remembered it from their one night together, and it brought back a rush of memories from that evening—the feel of his hands on her, his kisses, his moans of pleasure, his body wrapped around hers, inside her, making her feel cared for and precious and beautiful and treasured…

He pulled back, tiny splotches of crimson dotting his high cheekbones. "Sorry. Didn't mean to overstep there. I just…" He took a deep breath and looked up at her through his dark lashes, and even that was endearing, like basically everything else about him. "I'm very happy to hear that, Isabella. Thank you."

Okay. Awkward. Having a baby wasn't really something you thanked a person for, right? Though considering what she knew about him, she could see how he got there. "Um, you're welcome? I guess." Then, to get their day back on track, she said, "Are you ready to move on to the next spot on the list?"

"Why do you do that?" he asked, frowning.

"Do what?" A gust of wind blew, stronger this time, and she put a hand on her hat to keep it in place.

"Deflect."

"Deflect?" Now she scowled. "I'm not sure what you're talking about."

"I've told you a lot about my family, where I come from, what I'm here for, but each time I ask about you, I get nothing in return. You changed the subject fast. Don't you think that if we're going to be having a baby together, I should know more about you?"

"That's not true," she said, turning toward the view once more. "I told you about growing up the oldest kid, my mother passing away, then my dad getting sick and me having to take care of everyone. What more do you want to know?"

"Well, how about how all that made you feel?" He narrowed his gaze on her. "I want to know what makes you tick, Isabella Rivas. I want to know the inner you that you don't show to anyone else."

That all sounded very intimate and vulnerable and scared her half to death, frankly. Yes, they'd had sex, which some people might consider the most intimate thing two people could do together, but for Isabella that wasn't true. She'd spent the last twenty-one years learning to be self-reliant, learning to keep her emotions to herself to get done what she needed. To open up now, to Carlos, felt like jumping out of a plane with an iffy parachute. Maybe he'd catch her fall, maybe he wouldn't, but she couldn't find out without taking a leap of faith.

After a beat or two, she took a deep breath for courage, then nodded. "Fine. What do you want to know? And can we walk and talk at the same time? Because we've still got a lot of ground to cover today."

CHAPTER FIVE

BY THAT EVENING, they'd been to three more spots on his parents' whirlwind romance tour, including the Park Güell, the gorgeous Palau de la Música Catalana and the Parc del Laberint d'Horta or Labyrinth Park, where his parents had shared their last kiss before saying goodbye forever.

Now, tired and feet sore, they were dining in a charming restaurant called Jardinet d'Aribau. It was unlike any place Carlos had ever eaten before—a blend of fairy tale and fantastical, with lots of bright pastel colors and plants and vines growing wild around them. Like dining in a wonderland. Then again, he'd kind of felt like he'd been in a dream all day. Touring the city with Isabella had been everything he'd hoped for and more. He'd expected they'd get to know each other better. What he hadn't expected was for their connection to grow even stronger. And though she didn't mention it, he could tell from the way Isabella watched him when she thought he wasn't looking that she felt it, too. More than just desire. Or the baby. No. This felt like something deeper, stronger, richer. Something that might last if they allowed it to. Carlos wasn't sure how he felt about that yet.

"So," he asked, picking up his menu. "What's good here?"

"No idea." He raised a brow, and she laughed, the sound washing over him like fine music. "This is my first time here, too. But I've always wanted to try it."

"Ah." He smiled. "We are both new arrivals in this instance. Good."

When the server returned with their drinks—sangria for him, sparkling water for Isabella—they asked about the specials, then both decided on the blackened salmon with baby chard salad and a basket of Iberian ham and bread with tomato for an appetizer. Left alone once more, Carlos settled back in his seat, his feet brushing Isabella's beneath their cozy table for two in the corner.

"Thank you again for taking me out." He sipped his sangria, enjoying the cool, fruity taste. "It really helped make the pages of my mother's diary come alive for me. I can see why you love this city so much. It's beautiful."

"You're welcome." She smiled, seemingly much more open now than before. "Barcelona *is* beautiful. I wouldn't want to live anywhere else in the world."

"What was it like, growing up here?" he asked, skirting around the issue that had made her shut down earlier. He was still so interested in her and her past. He wanted to know more.

Isabella sighed then leaned forward, resting her elbow on the table, swirling her straw in her water. She looked tired but happy, and he hoped he hadn't worn her out too much. "Good. My family had a house in the Sarriá-Sant Gervasi district. Nothing fancy and far too small for all of us, but we were happy there. Lots of outdoor space to explore and safe neighborhoods. There were a lot of expat families living there, too, because it was close to the international schools. Our father was a handyman. He fixed electrical and plumbing, did construction, all of it. Made a good living doing it, too, at least until he got sick." She sighed and sat back, and for a moment

Carlos feared she'd close him off again. But then she continued, and he gave an internal sigh of relief. Perhaps she'd come to trust him after all. He hoped so, anyway.

"I think my mother's passing hurt him very deeply. He would never talk about it much, always trying to be strong for the rest of us, but it ate away at him, inside. Perhaps that's why he got sick." She gave a little shrug, staring at her water glass instead of Carlos, still stirring, stirring, stirring. "They say a patient's mental state has as much to do with their disease process and recovery as the physical medicine."

Carlos nodded. "I believe that, too, with my mother's cancer."

She glanced up at him then, the vulnerability in her eyes making his chest ache for her. "*Si.* I think after my mother died, something in my father's spirit went with her. His symptoms from MS gradually worsened and worsened until he could barely get out of bed. He couldn't work anymore, hardly ate. Like he wanted to join her in death. We were all sad, but he was grief-stricken."

The server came with their appetizers and to refill their drinks.

They each took a plate and filled it with

ham and fresh-baked bread and ripe tomatoes from the basket, then began to eat.

"I won't lie," Isabella said after a few minutes. "At the time, being thirteen and all, I took it personally."

"What?" Carlos asked, frowning.

"His withdrawal from us." She shrugged, eating another bit of bread and tomato before continuing. "I mean, looking back, I can't imagine the pressure he was under, trying to deal with all us kids and his work and everything else on his plate. But at the time, it was hard for me, losing my mother at that age. Then, when he got sick and I had to take over running the household, things only got worse."

"Couldn't he have hired someone to come in and help?" Carlos sipped more sangria, watching her over the rim. She'd let him in now, and he couldn't get enough. Wanted to keep her sharing if possible. "Or wasn't that an option?"

"No. Not really. Without his handyman work to support us, money was very tight. Luckily, he'd built up enough of a nest egg in savings to pay for the basics until I was old enough to get an after-school job to help supplement things, but we had to watch every penny."

She sighed and pushed aside her empty appetizer plate. "And at that time, the youngest ones were still barely walking, so, yeah. Not much of a life for me outside of cooking and cleaning and caring for everyone else in the family outside of school."

"Wow." He shook his head and sat back as the server came to clear their plates and refill their drinks again. Once they were alone again, Carlos reached over and took Isabella's hand, and she let him. "Well, as I've said, I'm sorry you went through that, but it explains why you're so strong and resilient."

"Hmm." She flashed a sad little smile. "Forged in fire, right?"

"Sometimes that's the only way."

Their dinners came then, and they stopped talking for a while—well, about anything other than the delicious food. The salmon was cooked to perfection and the chard salad its perfect cool, crispy complement. After they were full and happy, they paid the bill and walked back outside. The sun had set, and cooler air moved in off the ocean. Stars twinkled in the sky above, and people milled about, laughing and talking, out for a good time.

"Well, I guess it's back home, then," Carlos said, not wanting the evening to be over yet but not wanting to push his luck, either.

"Actually—" Isabella checked her smart watch. "There's one more spot I can show you tonight, if you're up for it."

"Always." He grinned, feeling that connection between them vibrate stronger, like a tuning fork, pulling him closer, keeping him in perfect resonance with her. "I'm yours."

Her dark eyes widened slightly at the innuendo of his words, then she grinned right back at him, taking his hand and tugging him alongside her down the cobblestoned street. Awareness zinged up his arm and straight down to his groin. Could've been the sangria. Could've been the woman leading him away to who knew where. Could've been the magnificent city around them. He felt free and fantastic and laser focused all at the same time. Mainly on Isabella and how her hips swayed so enticingly under her yellow sundress.

"Hurry," she said, looking back at him over her shoulder, her long dark hair swishing down her back, her sun hat long tucked away in the tote. "We'll miss the show."

"What show?" he asked just before they

rounded another corner, and boom. The view took his breath away. Just ahead, past a sea of tourists, a huge fountain sat atop a slight hill, spraying high into the sky, multicolored from the lights inside, in time to music playing from speakers set around it. Dazzling. "That's...wow!"

"It's called the Magic Fountain of Montjuïc," she said. "It's in the diary, too."

They stood watching the show, pressed close together to avoid being separated by the other tourists around them, holding hands because...well, because it felt so good. Carlos spotted a rose vendor off to the side of the fountain and excused himself a moment. They were all over the city, eager to make a buck off people looking to be romantic. He paid the guy and pointed toward Isabella, easy to spot in her bright dress, then made his way back to her to watch more of the show.

A sweet rendition of "The Way You Look Tonight" started playing when the rose man came over. "*Per a la dama,*" he said, giving a deep bow while holding out a single red rose to her.

Isabella frowned. "Oh, that's not for me."

"*Si,*" the rose man insisted. "It's for you."

She looked at Carlos. "Did you buy this?"

"What? Me? No." He shook his head, praying the rose vendor would keep going along with the ruse he'd planned. He'd thought it might be the perfect ice breaker to get things moving in the right direction again, because damn. Carlos had been dying to kiss her all day, and more than just the little peck he'd given her earlier. Still, he didn't want to be obvious about it, especially if she wasn't feeling the same about him. And sure, they'd already slept together, and he thought she might be into him, too, but he wanted to be sure. When Isabella hesitated, he squeezed her hand gently. "Go ahead. Take it."

"Well..." Her gorgeous smile rivaled the beautiful fountains in front of them. "If you insist."

"I do." Carlos gave the vendor a sly wink, and he returned it, then moved on to the next customer, leaving them alone again. "A pretty flower for a pretty woman."

In the glow from the fountains, he could see her blush slightly as she sniffed the rose. "Thank you."

"I didn't..." he started, then shrugged. "You're welcome."

Through her lashes, she looked up at him. "I hope it's not too much, all the things I told you at dinner. I don't usually say all that to people, but…"

"No, no. I'm glad you told me." He turned slightly to face her, reaching up to cup her cheek without even thinking. She didn't pull away. Her skin felt like silk beneath his touch, same as he remembered. Warm and smooth and addictive. His pulse tripped and blood pounded in his ears, drowning out the music and the people around them and everything but her. "I want to know more about you. I want to know everything about you, Isabella. And not just because of the baby."

"Really?" she said, staring into his eyes, a mix of hope and vulnerability there that made his chest ache. "I'm not very interesting."

"You're the most interesting thing in the world to me," he said, meaning it completely. And then time slowed as he bent toward her, close, closer, so close their breath mingled and he could smell the sweet fragrance of the rose in her hand and the scent of her shampoo. Then his lips brushed hers once, twice, before locking on. So good. Better than any kiss he'd ever had, even the night they'd slept together. Because now he knew her; now they were connected in a way they hadn't been before. Now, it meant something.

It meant everything.

Carlos slipped his arm around her waist and pulled her against him as he deepened the kiss. She opened to him, and he swept his tongue inside her mouth, tasting the spiciness of the salmon and the lemon from her water and something indefinably Isabella. She sighed and wrapped her arms around his neck, her soft curves pressing into his hard muscles, and the world felt perfect in that moment. Nowhere else he'd rather be than there with her that night. Perhaps his parents had been right. Perhaps Barcelona was the place to fall in love.

Isabella returned to work with Mario on the ambulance crew the next day, and the emergencies were coming fast and furious. In a way, she was glad. Not because people were getting hurt, but because it kept her from thinking too much about Carlos and their fabulous kiss.

After their one night together, she'd been firm in her decision to put it all behind her. Then she'd found out he worked at the hospital, and then that she was pregnant. Even then, she'd still been wary to let him too much into her life. She treasured her hard-earned freedom and had been prepared to raise the baby on her own. Then…

There'd been something about touring her city with him, showing him things his parents had done, that made her feel safe with him. After all, he'd showed her the diary and told her about his past. He'd made himself vulnerable. And while vulnerability was probably the scariest thing in the world to her, she trusted him. They hadn't known each other long, but something about Carlos made him seem steadfast and trustworthy. It's what made him so good at his job and good with his patients. That calm, cool collectedness. Like whatever happened, it would be okay.

She and Mario raced to another accident scene—this time a cyclist who'd been knocked off his bike near the boardwalk at the beach by a slow-moving motorist. When they pulled up to the scene, pandemonium ensued, as usual. The police were trying to cordon off the area while tourists swarmed around, filming it all with their smartphone cameras.

A woman and a man were standing nearby, talking with a police officer. Isabella took the man, leaned over, holding his gut. Mario took the woman, who was shaking and crying.

"Sir?" Isabella set her medical pack near her feet. "Are you all right? Can you tell me where it hurts?"

"I… I don't know." He shook his head, the sun reflecting off his dark green bike helmet. "It all happened so fast. My chest is kind of sore." He frowned and rubbed the area over his sternum. "I think I hit the handlebars of my bike when I fell off."

Right. Isabella got out her stethoscope and helped the man lean back against the police car parked behind him, then listened to his breathing and took his pulse. Both were normal. "Did you hit your head? Lose consciousness? Any shortness of breath? Irregular heartbeats? History of high blood pressure?"

"No. I didn't hit my head or black out." The man winced. "I'm pretty healthy overall. I ride my bike down here all the time. This is the first time anything like this has ever happened to me."

"Oh, God!" The woman driver's Southern American accent stood out sharply among all the Spanish speakers on the beach. "I'm so, so sorry. I tried to get my stupid GPS to show the right location and I glanced down for just a second and…"

Isabella finished an initial exam of the

man, then straightened. "I don't see any acute injuries, sir, but you should let us take you in and have a doctor check you out in the ER to be on the safe side." She inspected a cut on his forearm and a couple scrapes on his knee and leg where he'd landed on the ground. "If you get into the rig, I can bandage up those lacerations for you as well."

The man nodded, and Isabella led him around the back of the ambulance, then helped him inside. Soon Mario joined them, with the woman who'd hit the cyclist. She appeared close to hyperventilating now. He guided the woman into the other seat and helped her put her head between her legs to keep her from passing out.

"Ma'am," Mario said in English, "please calm down. Everything will be fine. I'm going to check your blood pressure now, okay? Are you on any medications?"

She shook her head, and he wrapped the cuff around her arm, then inflated it before slowly releasing the air as he listened with his stethoscope. "One thirty-two over eighty-nine."

"Is that good or bad?" the woman asked.

"Good." Isabella concentrated on the wound she was treating on her patient's arm. Considering how bad things could have been on this run, everyone involved had been lucky. She talked to the man to distract him from the sting of the antiseptic she used. "Hydrogen peroxide doesn't really disinfect things, like many people think. Only cleans it out a bit." She finished with the gauze, then tossed it into the biohazard bin beside her before applying more clean gauze pads atop the cut and wrapping it all in an ACE bandage. "Okay. Sir, have you decided if you want us to take you in?"

The man frowned at his arm, then at the scratches on his legs before shaking his head. "No. I think I'm okay, really. Has anyone checked my bike?"

"I did," Mario said. "It's fine. Put it against the front of the rig to keep it out of the way."

"Then no." The man ran his hand through his dark hair, still a mess from being under his helmet and sweaty. "I don't need to go."

Isabella had him sign a waiver refusing transport to the hospital, then gave him a card with all the information for St. Aelina's in case he changed his mind or required treatment later. By then, Mario had gotten the lady calmed down as well, and she looked much better. They sent both patients on their way before heading back toward headquarters to await another call.

They didn't have to wait long. Mario had barely turned into the parking lot when the dispatcher's voice rang through their radio and they got called out on a three-year-old boy with difficulty breathing. Within minutes they pulled up to the scene and climbed the stairs to the second floor to find the little boy on the sofa and his anxious mother nearby.

"Hello," Isabella said, moving to crouch in front of the boy, her medical pack at her feet, while Mario talked with the mother. He was on the small side for his age, wearing an orange-and-black knit cap on his head and a red-and-white-striped shirt with jean shorts. His little feet were bare. She smiled at him. "My name's Isabella. What's yours?"

"Barto," his mother said from her position near the sofa.

"Hello, Barto." Isabella pulled out her stethoscope and hung it around her neck. "Can I listen to your lungs?"

The little boy eyed her warily, wheezing.

"It won't hurt, I promise." She held the end of the stethoscope. "I'll just put this against your chest and listen."

Barto seemed to think about that, then nodded.

"Okay. Good." She leaned in and to check his lungs as Mario questioned the mother.

"When did his symptoms start?"

"Last night," the mother said. "I tried a humidifier and menthol rub on his chest along with his asthma meds, but it's only gotten worse."

Isabella sat back and nodded. "Sounds like croup."

As if in confirmation, Barto gave a hacking, wet cough.

"Oh, no." The mother's voice quivered.

"It'll be okay, ma'am." Mario patted her on the arm. "We're here, and we'll make sure your son gets the care he needs."

"Are you the police?" Barto asked Isabella.

"No." She grinned, then attached a pulse oximeter to the little boy's finger. "Not the police. Why? Are you under arrest?"

"No," Barto said, shaking his head, wide-eyed.

So cute. Reminded her of her younger brother Luis when he'd been that age. Isabella got out her pediatric blood pressure cuff next and held it up. "Can I see your arm?" The little boy extended it, and she put the cuff on. "Have you ever had your blood pressure checked, Barto?" He shook his head. "No? Okay. Well, this cuff is going to squeeze your arm a little bit, but that's all. Good. Relax your arm for me. There you go." She inflated the cuff, then slipped her stethoscope beneath the edge, listening for his heart sounds. "There you go. Great. You're doing amazing, Barto!"

The pulse oximeter beeped, and Isabella exchanged glances with Mario. The kid would need oxygen to help him breathe. His lips were already turning a bit blue.

"All right, big man," Isabella said, taking off the blood pressure cuff and keeping her tone cheerful. "We're going to give you a mask to wear. It will help you breathe better, okay, Barto?"

The boy balked a bit as Mario approached him with the clear oxygen mask. Isabella took it from her partner and held it in front of the little boy. "Here, it goes over your nose and mouth like this." She held it to her own face to show him. "There's medicine in there, too, to help you feel better. Take a deep breath in. Can you do that for me?"

Barto stared at the mask, his expression curious, then he reached a tentative hand for it. Isabella helped him hold it in front of his face, her eyes locked on him the whole time. "There you go. Breathe it in. That's right. In and out. In and out. Can you hold it there by yourself?"

He nodded.

"Excellent." Isabella stood and stuffed her gear back into her medical kit. "Barto, are you ready to go to the hospital now?"

"No," the little boy said. Everyone laughed.

"Come on," Isabella said, straightening. "It'll be fun. You'll ride with us. Your mother will be with you the whole time, okay?" She glanced at the mother and smiled. "Barto, do you want your mother to carry you out to the ambulance?"

"Yes, please."

"Okay." Mario stepped in. "Barto, I'm going to secure the mask to you with this strap, so you don't have to hold it anymore, all right?"

The little boy nodded. "Will it hurt?"

"Not at all." Mario got him taken care of, then stepped back. "There you go. You look like a dragon now. Want to be a dragon?"

Barto nodded.

"Cool." He gave the little boy a high five. "You're a dragon now."

They walked outside and waited while the mother got her purse and Barto, then locked up her flat before she joined them downstairs on the sidewalk. Once they helped them inside the back of the rig, Isabella joined them in back while Mario drove them to St. Aelina's.

Isabella took the opportunity to fill in more questions about the boy's history. "You said he had a fever?"

"Yes. Last night. It started at one zero two but then went up to one zero four."

"And did you give him anything to bring it down?"

"Acetaminophen," the mother said.

"Good." Isabella made her notes on her tablet. Barto looked to be feeling better, but they were taking him in to the ER anyway to have him evaluated. Protocol with the boy's asthma. He'd calmed now and the medication they gave him through the oxygen mask had lessened his cough. Dr. Santiago Garcia was on call tonight, if Isabella remembered correctly, so Barto and his mother would be in good hands.

A small tingle went through her as she realized she'd get to see Carlos again, too. They hadn't seen each other much today, and she missed him. Isabella smiled to herself. He was a good man, and they had a lot in common. They clicked well, and not just that one night they'd had together. She liked talking with him, spending time with him. She wasn't ready to call it more than a good friendship yet, but maybe she could see them getting there. Maybe.

They pulled into the ambulance bay at the hospital a few minutes later and took Barto inside. Sure enough, Carlos and Dr. Garcia, pediatrician, met them at the doors.

"What have we got?" Dr. Garcia asked as they led the boy and his mother down a hallway to an open exam room.

"His name is Barto," Isabella said, giving him the rundown. "He's three years old, history of asthma. Started having a wet, hacking cough last night and fever of up to one hundred and four. His O2 sats were low, and we started him on oxygen and corticosteroids."

"Very good." Dr. Garcia waited until the mother sat on the exam table, little Barto on her lap, before wheeling a stool up in front of them and taking a seat. "Hello, Barto. My name is Dr. Garcia. I'm going to help take care of you now, all right?"

Barto nodded, his head against his mother's chest.

Other staff filtered in, including Carlos, and Isabella caught his eye from across the room. They shared a little private smile before Carlos got to work on setting up a room for the boy.

"Okay, Barto. We're going to get started here," Dr. Garcia said, focusing on his patient and the mother. "A lot of people are going to be in here, doing different things, but I just want you to keep on taking those big breaths in and out for me while I listen to your chest..."

Isabella and Mario left the room and wandered back to the ambulance bay. Mario climbed into the back of the rig to clean up and restock while Isabella headed back inside. "I'm going to get something to drink from the cafeteria. Want anything?"

"Nope. I'm good, thanks," Mario said. "I'll text you if another run comes in."

"Thanks. Be right back."

She went downstairs to the cafeteria and got a bottled water, went back to the lobby, then took a seat in the atrium, where she could see Mario and the ambulance through the window in case they got another run. She felt a bit odd. Not sick, really, just…nostalgic, maybe. Seeing little Barto earlier had stirred up things inside her. Old memories and new fears. She realized she'd have a little son or daughter of her own soon, and while she was happy about the pregnancy, she was also scared. Scared she might mess things up. Scared that she might not be a good mother. Scared being a mother might be all she'd ever be…

"Hey," Carlos said, taking the seat beside her. She'd been so lost in her thoughts she hadn't even heard him arrive. He looked good, as always. Even the green scrubs he wore seemed custom made to flatter him, the color making his tanned skin look more bronzed, his dark eyes sparkle more, his voice deeper, sexier.

Okay, maybe that last one was her, but still.

She straightened in her seat and gulped down some water, glad for the coolness on her parched throat. "Hey."

Then he reached over and took her hand, and wow. Her pulse sped and her knees tingled. She had it bad for this guy, and that wasn't good. She couldn't bolt, though. Not here, where people knew her. She didn't want to cause a scene, so she stayed put, enjoying the warm press of his hand on hers far more than she should.

"How are you?" he asked, his thumb stroking small circles on her palm, reminding her all over again of their kiss the other night.

"Good," she said, the word squeaking out. She coughed and drank more water, than tried again. "Good. Thanks. Just tired."

"You aren't working too hard, are you?" His dark brows knit, his dimples disappearing beneath a frown. He leaned a bit closer to whisper, "You should rest more, with the baby."

His soft, minty breath tickled her cheek, and if she hadn't been sitting, Isabella believed she would've swooned. Which wasn't like her at all. If she'd been on the beach, she'd have taken her board and dived headfirst into a whitecap to get away. Now, she had to endure this sweet torture.

Rather than give in to her urge to snuggle closer to him, she turned to irritation instead. She hated being babied. Tugged on her hand in his, but he didn't let go. "I'm fine."

"Hmm." He watched her curiously. "I didn't mean to upset you."

She harrumphed, feeling prickly and out of sorts.

Carlos, charming as ever, darn him, just chuckled, continuing to stroke her palm like she was a wild horse he was trying to tame. He stared down at their joined hands, his expression unreadable. "You take care of others but don't like them taking care of you." He glanced up and caught her gaze. "You've told me a bit about your past, but not all. Why is it you don't like to be taken care of?"

For a moment, she considered getting up and walking away. But something kept her there, in her seat. Something warm and wild and far too scary for her to want to think about just then. She tried to shake his question off with a nonanswer. "I don't know. I guess it's a carryover from my job."

"Hmm." He sat back, blinking at her. "Which one?"

She frowned. "What do you mean?"

"Well, it seems to me you have two jobs. The one you work now, as a paramedic. And the one you left behind when your siblings moved out."

Wow. She'd known he was very empathetic, but no one had ever gotten her so well, so quickly. Too stunned to deny it, she just nodded. "That's true."

Carlos nodded, then slowly brought her

hand to his lips to kiss the back of it gently. Mesmerized, she didn't even care that the staff behind the desk across the way were probably staring at them. She never intended to talk about any of this, especially here at work, but no one else was around them, and even in the large atrium, things between her and Carlos felt very cozy and intimate.

"I'm the caretaker. I've always been the caretaker," she said, her tone hushed as memories flooded back. "Ever since our mom passed, as the eldest, I had to take over. I cared for my younger siblings and then also my father after he got sick. I had to stay strong for them. I did stay strong for them."

"You did," he murmured, tucking her hand against his chest, right over his heart. His scrub shirt had slipped down a little so her bare skin brushed his and, oh, Lord. All the oxygen disappeared from the room. She gulped in a breath, blood pounding in her ears. It was too much. It wasn't enough. "You were so strong, *hermosa*. You still are. Strong, independent, beautiful."

His pulse beat in time with hers beneath her touch, and their gazes locked. The world shifted beneath her, and in that moment, Isabella realized that no matter how things turned out with Carlos, her life would never be the same. "I must be careful," he said, and there were those dimples again, drawing her further under his spell. "You could steal my heart, *hermosa*. And we can't have that."

She watched him, eyes half-closed, unable to move, unable to breathe, unable to do anything except lean closer to him. Somewhere in the back of her mind, caution alarms went off, but she ignored them.

At least until her phone buzzed in her uniform pocket.

Carlos sat back and she fumbled for her phone, pulling it out to see a text from Mario saying they had another call to go out on. She didn't dare look out the window to where her EMT partner stood for fear of seeing the knowing look on his face.

Dammit.

She stood and finished her water before tossing the bottle in the nearby recycle bin, saying a silent prayer for small miracles. If she wasn't careful, Carlos wouldn't be the only one losing his heart here.

"I, uh, need to get back to work," she said, face hot and scalp tingling.

"What about dinner? Tomorrow night?" he asked, following her to the ambulance bay doors. “We can get a table at my uncle’s place, near the back. Talk more, have some good food. Just relax.”

Isabella knew she had a choice to make then, and her rational brain wanted to say no. Being around him made her forget everything else, and that was too seductive and dangerous. But the other part of her all but tumbled over itself to say yes before she could stop herself. “Fine. Text me the time. I’ll meet you there.”

Then she walked out the door as fast as her feet could carry her. Running to an emergency or away from another, she couldn’t really say.

CHAPTER SIX

THE NEXT EVENING, Carlos stood on the side-walk outside Encanteri, waiting for Isabella. Excitement and anticipation buzzed through his bloodstream, making him antsy. Several groups of tourists and locals stood nearby, chatting and laughing, but Carlos couldn't concentrate on anything but the woman he feared he'd fallen for too hard and too fast.

After all, they'd only spent a few hours together, touring the sights of the city, getting to know each other better. And yes, they'd slept together once already, but that had been a while ago, and now he started to wonder if it had all been a dream. Well, no. Not a dream, since Isabella was pregnant with his baby, but still.

What had happened to him with his father had left him shaken, and he was hesitant of relationships in general and didn't like to label things. Labels were bad, in his opinion. He'd dealt with enough of them in his life. But this thing with Isabella wasn't going away. In fact, their connection seemed stronger than ever, and the more he learned about her, the more he wanted to know. Unsettling, that.

And if her phone hadn't gone off the day before in the lobby, he would've kissed her right there in his workplace, which wasn't like him. He never lost control of his emotions. He felt for his patients, yes, of course. But never did he let those feelings rule him or override his judgment. Only with Isabella. A problem indeed.

"Sorry I'm late," she said, rushing up to him at the curb, looking stunning in another sundress. This one light pink and purple, like the sunset above them. "An older neighbor caught me on the way out of my building and wanted to chat. I didn't want to be rude."

"I understand," he said, and he did. Many times, the older patients in the ER just wanted company, someone to talk to, and Carlos was happy to be that person for them. He considered the contact part of his job every bit as important as the medicine.

They went inside, and Carlos managed to flag down his uncle, who worked behind the bar, helping one of the bartenders with some complicated contraption for mixing drinks that looked like it came straight out of Dr. Frankenstein's lab. Lots of bubbling beakers and metal pipes and brightly colored test tubes.

"Wow. I'd forgotten how pretty this place was inside."

"It is, isn't it?" Carlos smiled, looking around. All the sparkling glass and carved woodwork, bottles and bits and bobs. A feast for the eyes as well as the palate. A low hum of conversation bounced off the rough-hewn stone walls, and streetlights glimmered through the arched stained-glass windows at the front. The mood felt casual and cool, and Carlos felt incredibly proud of his uncle's accomplishments here at the bar. Family meant everything to him after growing up without part of his. He never wanted his own child to experience that. Another reason to tread carefully with Isabella. He didn't want to mess up the coparenting thing with a messy romance, even if the prospect grew more tempting by the second.

His uncle wove through the crowded bar over to them, still smiling broadly. "Nephew," he said, kissing Carlos on both cheeks, then did the same to Isabella. Cubans were very warm people. "And Isabella. Don't you look lovely this evening."

She did, too. All long legs and smooth skin, and Carlos did his best not to notice. A failed effort. He couldn't not notice Isabella, it seemed. From the moment she was near, he knew it from the tingle in his skin, the thud of his pulse. Something primal and undeniable and, oh, boy. Not good. Not good at all.

"Did you save us a table, Uncle?" Carlos asked, hoping to move things along.

"Of course, nephew." He linked arms with Isabella, leading her away toward the back of the bar, leaving Carlos behind to trail after them. Through the din of talk around them, he made out his uncle telling her Carlos got impatient sometimes when nervous and she would have to see what she could do about that. Isabella laughed then, the sound musical and light, and he found himself becoming enchanted all over again. Ridiculous. Insane. Like drinking expensive, heady madeira straight from the bottle and he wasn't sure he'd ever get enough.

They finally stopped near a small table for two in the back corner near the windows. Candles flickered from the center of the table, and a bowl of red and pink roses completed the centerpiece. His uncle helped Isabella with her chair, then handed them each a menu. Isabella ordered sparkling water to drink, and Carlos got cava. "If I may suggest, nephew, let me pick your entrées tonight. The chef had made something very special just for you two."

"Oh." Carlos glanced at Isabella to find her wide-eyed and smiling. "I'm game if you are."

"Sure."

They turned in their menus to his uncle, who bowed slightly, a glint in his eyes. "Very good. I'll be back shortly with your appetizers and drinks."

Once they were alone, Isabella fiddled with her napkin while Carlos took an inordinate interest in the street outside. Finally, she said, "I didn't know your uncle Hugo waited tables, too."

"Oh, he doesn't. Usually. He just wants to keep an eye on us." Carlos grinned. "He's very nosy."

"He cares for you a lot." Isabella straightened her silverware next. "That's obvious."

"I care for him, too. He's the only family I have here."

Hugo brought their drinks, along with a basket of deviled crab croquettes and *bolitas de yuca*. "Enjoy," his uncle said before quickly departing, and now Carlos's suspicions rose. Both appetizers were distinctly Cuban in origin.

"Wow," Isabella said, putting one of each of the deep-fried, breaded balls onto her plate. "What are they?"

"These—" Carlos pointed to a croquette "—are deviled crab balls and should be eaten with the cocktail sauce there. And the other ones are *tostones*. Both Cuban delicacies. And safe during pregnancy, as they've been cooked properly. In fact, the plantains in the *tostones* are an excellent source of folates. The sauce for those is avocado, lime and garlic. It's called *mojo verde*."

"Hmm." She dipped one of the round, smashed, fried green plantains in the bowl of green sauce beside it, then took a bite. "Wow! That's so good. I've never had Cuban food before."

"Well, I'm glad to be your first, then." He gave her a saucy little wink. "And yes, they are very good." He spooned out some sauce onto his own plate and put some more on hers as well. "The *mojo verde* really brings out all the flavors."

They both ate a few bites of each. For Carlos it felt like a bit of home, which he suspected was his uncle's whole plan. He might have mentioned how much he liked Isabella to his uncle and how much he wished he could show her his homeland. Knowing Uncle Hugo, this was an invitation to bring Cuba here, when Carlos couldn't just leave and go to Cuba.

"How is everything so far?" his uncle asked, returning to refill their drinks.

"Well, seeing as how it's all gone, I'd say it's going well." Carlos leaned in to whisper, "Thank you."

"Wait until you see what's next, *sobrino*." His uncle waggled his brows, then cleared away their empty plates. "Your dinner will be ready shortly."

Carlos waited until they were alone again, pleasantly full and relaxed a bit more now, thanks to the cava. He'd been wanting to pick up their conversation from the day before in the lobby but hadn't known how to start. Maybe, if Isabella felt more comfortable, too, he could ease into it now. Deep down, instinct told him there was more in her past that kept her from moving forward.

"So." He smiled across the table at her, their legs tangling slightly beneath the table. Neither of them pulled back. A good sign in his book. "Tell me more about your family growing up."

Isabella shrugged, smoothing the tablecloth with her hand. She did that, he'd noticed, whenever she was uncomfortable. Cleaning things up, straightening them. Like trying to form order out of chaos. His heart tugged a little more toward her. If he wasn't careful, it would belong to her forever. He could blame his purple prose on the cava, but that would be a lie.

It wasn't all the drink.

"Not much to tell, really. Other than what I've already said."

"I don't believe you."

"I don't care." They stared at each other across the table, a standoff of sorts, and Carlos wished he hadn't blurted out those words like that, but dammit. His brain didn't seem to work when she was around. He was all feeling, all emotion. One big, raw, vulnerable nerve ending vibrating for her touch. He hoped she wouldn't get up and walk away. He prepared for the worst anyway. Her dark eyes sparkled with hurt and hesitation, like a fawn ready to race away at the slightest movement. Carlos stayed still, watching, waiting.

Then his uncle returned with a tray of delicious-smelling food, saving the evening. "Here we are, compliments of the chef."

As his uncle set out plate after plate of Cuban delicacies, Carlos's chest warmed even more. "*Tío*, what did you do?"

"I brought you a little bit of home," he said in Spanish. "I knew you were feeling a bit homesick lately and thought it would be a nice surprise for you and your lady friend."

Carlos stood to kiss his uncle on the cheek, then beamed over at Isabella, their earlier tension forgotten. "Tonight, you shall taste my homeland."

Her small smile grew, the wariness in her eyes disappearing beneath a sparkle of happiness. "I can't wait. I'm starving."

He almost made a comment about her eating for two but caught himself at the last minute. They'd agreed not to say anything yet until she'd told her family, and he didn't want to ruin things now that they were back on track.

Carlos waited until his uncle had laid everything out, then told her the name of each dish. "This is *ropa vieja*, Cuban-style shredded beef. Next, we have *fricasé de pollo*, or Cuban-style chicken stew, and finally there's *pernil asado con mojo*, marinated pork shoulder roast. Again, all cooked properly, so safe for you and the baby. On the side is rice and beans and more *tostones*. Plus, extra *mojo verde* to dip it all in."

"I..." She blinked at all the food, then back at him. "I'm not even sure where to start."

Carlos sighed and reached over for her hand. "How about over again? I'm sorry for my stupid question before. I didn't mean to put you on the defensive."

Isabella shook her head, staring down at her plate. "I'm sorry, too. I... My past is a touchy subject sometimes."

"I get that." He winked once more, then dished up food for them both. "Let's eat. We can talk later."

They dined and chatted, the tension easing away with good food and conversation, until, about halfway through the meal, Isabella sighed. "I wish I could be more open about growing up," she said, and he froze midbite, not wanting to move in case she stopped talking again. "But I don't know. I always get tangled up." She pushed a bite of rice around on her plate with her fork, not looking at him, brows drawn together. "I think maybe it's guilt."

"Guilt?" he said, too shocked to stay silent. "What would you have to feel guilty about?"

"I guess I always wonder if I could've done more to help my father. If I did enough for my siblings." She snorted softly. "Or maybe if I did too much and smothered them. Maybe that's why they all moved out and away as soon as they were able. Away from me."

"Oh, Isabella," he said, reaching across to take her hand. "I'm sure you did everything you could. You were just a child yourself. It's not your fault. None of that was your fault."

She shrugged, looking unconvinced. "Maybe. And I did do my best, but none of them had any idea how hard it was for me back then. They were all too small to understand. Then when they were older and left me behind to pursue their dreams, I was happy for them. But I was also hurt."

She shook her head. "Even Diego got married to Grace in the UK and didn't even invite his family." Isabella straightened and pushed her plate away, wiping her mouth with her napkin and still avoiding his gaze. "I mean,

I know Father's death was inevitable, but I can't shake the feeling that I could have done more, should have done more to keep us all together after he passed. But then I also feel guilty for wanting escape myself sometimes. It's complicated."

She finally met his gaze, and he wanted nothing more than to hold her close and tell her everything would be all right. "I'm not sure why I told you all that. I feel like I've been running from those emotions for a long time. But somehow you make it okay for me to talk."

Carlos felt like his heart had swelled to fill his whole chest. He swallowed hard and squeezed her hand tighter. "I'm glad you can talk to me, *hermosa*. I want to be there for you, and not just because of the baby."

She smiled then, warm and sweet, tightening her hold on his hand. "Thank you. That means a lot to me." She lowered her head again, taking a deep breath. "I've stayed busy for years, using it as a distraction. It's probably why I like being a paramedic so much. The adrenaline rush, the fact that it's nomadic in a way. Always something new and different. Never the same thing twice. Never stuck in one spot. Not getting too attached."

"Oh, *hermosa*," he said, the words emerging gruff due to his constricted throat. "I'm sorry for—"

Isabella held up a hand, stopping him, her smile sad. "No, please. Don't feel sorry for me. That only makes it worse. I like my life. I'm happy. I never wanted to settle down after what happened to my parents." She shook her head. "Never thought a child would be on my agenda at all. Not after what felt like a lifetime of responsibility and my sense of failure after that." She took a deep breath, the beat stretching out between them, taut and tender. "But then I met you, and you changed things. Not just the baby, Carlos. When I'm not with you, I don't feel like a confident, independent woman. I feel alone."

He did get up then, couldn't help it, and pulled her into his arms. Except they were blocking an important aisle, so he pulled her out onto the dance floor instead. A small band had set up in the corner playing standards, and they'd begun a slow song. He held Isabella against him, letting her know without words that he supported her. He'd always be there for her, no matter what. As the music washed over them, she gradually relaxed against him and they swayed gently to the music, first one song, then another, then another, until Carlos lost track of time, of their location, of everything except the woman in his arms and the incredible things she made him feel.

Eventually, he looked over to find his uncle Hugo clearing their table, watching them dance with a fond smile. He gave Carlos a grin and a thumbs-up, and Carlos nodded back. His uncle had become a surrogate father, and he loved him for it. But right now, there were more important things on his mind. He wanted more time with Isabella—all night, if she'd let him.

He pulled away slightly, to meet her gaze, soft and sweet in the dim light. A simple question, but it felt like the most important one he'd ever asked. "Come upstairs with me, *hermosa*? We don't have to do anything. Just talk, if you like. But I don't want this night to end. Not yet." *Not ever.*

She watched him a long moment, then raised a hand to trace her fingers down his cheek, making him shiver. An answering yearning lit her eyes, making his pulse notch higher and his blood sing. "I don't want it to end, either, Carlos."

They kissed, and his world rocked. He

grabbed her hand and pulled her back to the table for a quick goodbye to his uncle. She grabbed her bag, then they were out the door and climbing the stairs to his flat. His fingers trembled and he damned near dropped the keys, but finally they were inside and Isabella was in his arms and kissing him, tasting of spices and sweet desire.

They made their way down the hall to his bedroom, not breaking the kiss, a trail of discarded clothes in their wake, until they fell onto his bed, naked and desperate. Different than the first night they'd been together. Then it had been all about exploring, getting to know what the other liked. Now, it was hot and intense, their feelings making every touch, every sigh more meaningful.

Carlos kissed his way down to her breasts, cupping them in his palms, then taking one taut nipple into his mouth. Isabella cried out, little mewls shooting like lightning straight to his groin. She pulled him closer, needing more. He gave her everything, putting all his want and need and love into his caresses. More than sex. Way more, at least for him. They were making love in every sense of the word.

* * *

Isabella thought she'd died and gone to heaven when Carlos kissed his way down her body to her abdomen, then lower still, tracing his tongue over her slick folds. While she wasn't a virgin by any means, being with Carlos felt different from any lover she'd had before. Even their first time together. But before, it had felt heated and rushed and inquisitive. Now, she knew Carlos better, and it seemed to shed a new light on their lovemaking. His consideration and kindness extended to the bedroom this time as well, with him making sure she was comfortable and happy and satisfied before he took his own pleasure. He nuzzled and made love to her with his hands and mouth until she tumbled over the brink into orgasm, unable to keep from whispering his name over and over as the waves of ecstasy rocked her entire being.

At last, he kissed his way up her body again, stopping to nuzzle her breasts once more before propping himself up on one elbow while reaching into his nightstand drawer for a condom.

She stopped him. "We don't need that now, remember?"

Carlos froze, his eyes widening slightly as

her words sank in. They could be together tonight with nothing between them.

Heat prickled her cheeks then, making her suddenly shy. "I haven't been with anyone since you."

"Me neither." He blinked down at her. "Are you sure, though, *hermosa*?"

Isabella nodded. She couldn't wait to feel him inside her with no barrier between them at all and reached up to smooth away the sudden lines of tension etched near the corners of his mouth and eyes. Then she trailed her hand lower, stopping once she'd encircled his hard length, stroking him until Carlos pulled her hand away and kissed her palm. "Too much of that, *hermosa*, and I won't last."

In answer, she drew him down for an open-mouthed kiss while wrapping her legs around his waist and arching her hips into him. "Please, Carlos. I need you…"

He rose above her, holding his weight on his forearms, the tip of his hard length poised at her wet entrance. A beat passed, then two, before he finally entered her in one long stroke, then held still, allowing her body to adjust to his. When he did move at last, they both moaned deeply and began a rhythm that had them teetering on the brink in no time at all.

"Carlos, I..." Isabella cried out as she climaxed once more, her words lost as the universe exploded into a million iridescent shards around her. Maybe the pregnancy hormones made her more responsive. Maybe the magic of the night entranced her. Maybe they were so in sync, both in and out of bed, all her nerve endings twinkled like diamonds. Whatever it was, she felt like a live wire, sparking and shimmering with pleasure whenever he was near. He drove into her once, twice more, then his body tightened in her arms as he came hard inside her, his face buried in her neck and her name on his lips, murmuring sweet nothings against her skin.

Afterward, they lay in the darkness, listening to the crickets outside, his head resting in the valley between her breasts, over her heart, and her fingers in his hair, tracing lazy circles against his scalp. She felt sated and relaxed for the first time in a while, and she had Carlos to thank for that as well. Isabella opened her mouth to tell him so, but he raised up slightly to meet her gaze, speaking first as his frown returned, deepened.

"That...wow," he said, his voice quiet in

the shadows. "I don't know what this is happening between us, *hermosa*, but I want it to continue. I want to explore it more."

She couldn't really see his face in the dark, but the vulnerability in his tone made her heart clench. Isabella wanted that, too, even if it scared her. He rolled over onto his back and pulled her into his side, her leg sprawling across his and her head on his chest as he pulled the covers up over them. Beneath her hand, his pulse was steady and true. "I'd like that," she whispered.

"Good." He gathered her closer. "You know, I came here to retrace my parents' last steps together, but it seems I've begun a journey of my own—with you. History is repeating itself." He sighed, hesitated. "I only ever wanted to belong somewhere. To know I had a place, roots. I had half in Cuba, but today I found the rest. Perhaps you could be my roots here, *hermosa*."

She nodded, his words bittersweet. Roots meant staying in one place, and that's the thing she'd fought against most of her adult life. But she didn't want to ruin this moment, this one perfect evening together, so she kept that to herself. They'd have plenty of time to talk about it tomorrow.

"Hmm. This is nice, too," he said, his words rumbling beneath her ear, warm and deep. "I hope you enjoyed tonight. My uncle felt proud to serve you that dinner." He nestled her head under his chin, and she snuggled closer into his heat, meaning every word. It was wonderful. The food, the company. Everything.

"Good night, *hermosa*," Carlos said, kissing the top of her head before drifting off to sleep, and Isabella soon followed him into slumber.

CHAPTER SEVEN

"SINCE THIS IS your first time, let's practice on the sand before we hit the waves." Isabella nodded to two surfboards a few feet away that they'd hauled down from her flat earlier. It had been a week since they'd slept together at his place and the first time their work schedules had coordinated, so they were spending time together, getting to know each other better still by sharing things they loved. Today was Isabella's choice, so of course, they were surfing. Isabella had checked the weather forecasts earlier this morning before they'd left her flat, and thanks to some storms brewing out in the Atlantic from off the coast of western Africa, thousands of miles away, the conditions were perfect at Bogatell. Well, perfect for an experienced surfer like her, anyway.

"Okay." Carlos took off his T-shirt and

dropped it onto his beach towel next to his flip-flops and sunglasses. "Is that for me?" A black wet suit sat next to one of the boards.

"If you want it. The water's cold, but you get used to it quickly. Up to you."

"I'm good." He wanted to feel the salt water on his skin with as little barrier as possible, no matter how chilly it might be. With open-water swimming and surfing outlawed in his home country of Cuba for fear people would leave for good, it would be a relatively new experience. The only other time he'd been out in the water here was the first night he'd met Isabella, but with a man's life in their hands, his attention had obviously been elsewhere.

She smiled and led him to her board. "You've got sunscreen on, right?"

"*Si.*" He had a good base tan and he was olive skinned anyway, but still. One could never be too careful with the ultraviolet rays. Also, bringing along the stuff might give him a chance to get Isabella's hands on him again. "But..." He bent and picked up the bright yellow tube of sunscreen from his beach towel and held it out to her, not missing the way she checked him out. His skin tingled from more than the heat now.

"You didn't get your back," Isabella said,

taking the stuff from him and squirting it out in her hand before walking around behind him. Beneath his striped board shorts, his body tightened at the first cool touch of her hand on him. "How's that?"

Carlos nearly moaned, his eyes slipping closed as she rubbed the cream into the knotted muscles between his shoulder blades. "Good, *hermosa*," he managed to get out, the words rough with suppressed need. They couldn't do anything here, not with all the tourists and kids around, but man. He wanted to. Boy, did he want to. "That feels so good."

Tingles exploded through his body, and it took all his willpower not to turn and scoop Isabella into his arms and haul her back to her flat, caveman-style, to have his wicked way with her. His breath hitched as she leaned in, her fingers tickling the hair at the nape of his neck. Isabella was tall for a woman and fit him so perfectly inside and out, he still had to pinch himself sometimes to make sure all this was real. But then he finally inhaled deep and smelled her scent over the sand and the sea and knew this was real. She smelled like fresh flowers and tropical fruit from her sunscreen and warm, sweet woman. And now he ached from this very normal, casual act and, oh, boy.

Bring on the cold water.

Isabella lifted her hands away from him not a moment too soon.

Thankfully, for the next several minutes, Isabella gave him a lesson on surfing on land, which required a lot of lying down on the board, so his front was hidden. Uncomfortable? Yes. Necessary? Also, yes. Carlos did his best to pay attention to what she taught him and forget about his traitorous body, copying Isabella's movements as best he could and hoping the learning process was long enough to commit the movements to his muscle memory. His analytical brain might be hardwired better than most, but it was still hard to focus on the task at hand. Not when Isabella was there, too, and he could watch the strength and power in her supple, shapely arms and legs.

"I think you're ready," Isabella said at last, tucking her surfboard under her arm. "You good?"

Besides feeling like he'd just gone ten rounds with a prizefighter in the ring, yeah. Carlos gave her a thumbs-up. And prayed he wouldn't make a complete fool of himself out there.

The second the water reached his knees, his body shriveled in on itself and his breath caught in his chest, making it difficult to inhale. It wasn't that cold. Not really. It was June, after all, but the shock was still there. Exhales in rapid succession didn't help much, but Isabella's amiable voice did.

"Don't panic, *cariño.* You'll get used to it in a minute."

Maybe. But then the tide came at him with more force than he expected, and Carlos wavered.

Isabella moved the surfboard between them, obviously aware that he had issues keeping his balance on top of breathing normally. He knew how to swim. Had learned in his grandparents' pool in Havana. But the ocean was a whole different ball game. She pointed at the board, then him. "Hop on. I'll get us farther out."

Carlos maneuvered onto the board, getting into position on his stomach just like he'd been taught, and tried not to freak out. Probably watching Shark Week on streaming had been a mistake. Not to mention riptides. He heard about patients getting caught in those all the time in the ER. How deep did they have to go? His pulse revved.

A wave came at them, and Carlos squeezed his eyes shut as Isabella guided him over it. It splashed in his face, though, and he still managed to swallow a mouthful of the stuff before spitting it out.

"It helps to keep your mouth closed," Isabella said in a slightly snarky tone before winking at him.

So instead, he coughed and sputtered with his head tilted down, hoping not to draw too much attention to the fact he had no idea what he was doing. When they reached the strip of white water Isabella had mentioned during his beach training earlier, she spun his board around so that Carlos faced the shoreline.

From out here, the sand looked miles away. The gentle sway of the vast water made him hyperaware of his surroundings, and sudden fear plunged like a meteor deep into his gut. He understood now why the Cuban government warned people not to swim in the waters around the island. It would be too easy to be caught up and swept away. He grabbed Isabella's hand, ready to denounce all his machismo and say flat out he'd changed his mind.

But then he remembered the thrill of seeing

the city with her, how she'd looked the first night standing on the shore, so wistful and wonderful. And all he'd been through before coming to Barcelona and after.

As if reading his thoughts, Isabella leaned in and kissed his cheek, then whispered, "You can do this, *cariño*. Remember what I taught you."

Then everything happened so fast, and Carlos had no more time to think at all.

"Now, ready…set…go." Isabella gave him a push.

He paddled like mad to catch the wave. Way too fast, the tide rolled over him and he forgot all the things Isabella had taught him. The surfboard bounced beneath him, and water curled above his head and Carlos squeezed his eyes shut and seriously considered vomiting.

You can do this, cariño.

Isabella's voice in his head forced his eyes open, and he pushed up to his feet on the board, arms out for balance, and for a split second he did it, riding on the water, powerful and free and…

He toppled sideways.

Next thing he knew, the riptide tossed him feet over head and pulled him under. Without thinking, he opened his mouth and immediately swallowed more salty water, and his eyes stung. All his swimming skills meant nothing here and the more he struggled against the current, the harder it became, arms flailing like mad, legs kicking but getting him nowhere. His lungs screamed for air.

Then, in his head, Isabella's training came back to him. *Don't fight it. Go with the current if you go under.* Even though it went against his every instinct, Carlos stopped fighting and relaxed, all his muscles going slack, praying silently that he'd reach the surface soon.

Ten, nine, eight...

In a few more seconds, he'd run out of air. Swim. He needed to swim. Diagonal to the shore, except he had no idea of the direction. Then, by some miracle, warm sunshine bathed his face, and he gulped for air.

He'd made it. Exhausted from head to toe, but alive. He caught enough breath to yell out a weak "Help" before slipping back under the water. Arms wrapped around him then and pulled him above the surface once more. He breathed, more deeply than he ever had before, eyes closed because it was hard to keep them open. He felt himself being dragged forward through the water. Voices echoed around him, muffled and incoherent. A cool, hard surface met his back, and the warmth around him faded away. "Carlos? *Cariño.* Can you hear me?"

"Ye-yes," he whispered.

"Open your eyes." Isabella's voice had switched into professional paramedic mode now, though he knew her well enough to detect the edge of fear beneath.

It took a moment, but he finally managed to pry his eyes open and blink up into Isabella's face. A blurry crowd had gathered around them on the beach. Disoriented, Carlos pressed his palms into the wet sand and tried to sit up, blinking hard.

"Hey," Isabella said, putting her hand on his chest, forcing him back down to the sand. "You're okay. Just lie there a minute and breathe, okay? Just relax. You're safe now."

"Sorry," he croaked out, his throat sore from all the salt water he'd swallowed. "I did that wrong."

"*No te preocupis,*" she said in Catalan, smiling down at him, stroking the damp hair from his forehead. It felt good. Soothing. His breathing slowed along with his pulse. And maybe he'd been in Barcelona long enough now, or maybe he'd just been around Isabella enough, but he understood what she said much quicker than before. *No worries.* Sitting there with her, as she stroked his head, he had none.

A lifeguard pressed between two bystanders, asking in Spanish, "Everything all right here?"

"Fine," Isabella answered back. They started talking then, apparently knowing each other from her paramedic route. It all went over Carlos's head. His now-pounding head, but nothing a few pain relievers wouldn't banish. His muscles were sore now, too, from his struggle against the riptide.

Murmurs ran through the crowd around them, several different languages at once—Spanish, English, French, even some Japanese. Barcelona was a cosmopolitan city, after all. Carlos lay there, thinking how odd it was to be on the other side of things. Usually, he was the medical professional, handling the patient. Now the tables were turned. He was glad Isabella was there for him, even as he feared he might trigger her fears again. She'd spent so many years caring for others. He didn't want to be a burden. Like he'd been a burden to his mother and grandparents.

Okay. Maybe he was the one triggered now.

"Let's give him some space, please," Isabella said to the circle of people around them, authority in her tone. Seconds later, sunshine instead of shadows filled the airspace above her.

Carlos raised a hand to shield his eyes from the bright sun and squinted up at Isabella. "I'm okay."

This time when he started to sit up, she helped him, eventually taking his hand and helping him to his feet. His legs still felt a bit wobbly but held. He reached behind him to wipe the itchy sand off his board shorts.

"Want to try again?" Isabella asked.

"Uh…no. Thanks." Carlos snorted. "I think one humiliation is enough. But you go ahead and surf if you want. The waves still look good. Be careful, though. I don't want what happened to me to happen to you."

"Are you sure?" Isabella frowned, then glanced out at the water. He didn't miss the yearning in her expression. She loved this. Born for it. All those old fears surfaced again inside him before he tamped them down. Isabella bit her lip and met his gaze once more. "And I'll be fine. I've surfed much rougher conditions than this in my life. But we can go back if you prefer."

"No." Carlos shook his head and smiled. "Please, *hermosa*. I want you to enjoy yourself. I know you've missed this."

She sighed, then gave him an answering grin. "Yeah, I really have. If you're sure..."

"I am."

The crowd slowly dispersed, the show over, and Carlos stood there watching the woman he loved grab her surfboard and run straight for the water that had nearly just killed him, trying to figure out how they could be so different yet still make this work. For themselves, and for their child.

Isabella tried to be in the present, to lose herself in the water as she loved to do, as she done through her most difficult teen years. Because of the storms far out to sea, the waves were good sized, pounding the beach in the bright sunshine. Her pulse raced from a mix of residual fear for what had happened to Carlos and from the surge of adrenaline being this near to the ocean always gave her. She paddled out and caught a wave. Stood on her board, feeling the air rush past and the spray of water, the power of the eight- to ten-foot wave carrying her forward harder, faster. Making her forget everything—all the stress and doubts and longings—until nothing existed but her and water. Carlos had been concerned about her going out again after what had happened to him, but she'd waved it off. A risk, yes, but she was very experienced and could handle it.

Cursing herself under her breath for what had happened to Carlos, she turned around and paddled back out again to catch another wave and ride it in. Then another. And another. Hoping maybe the exertion would burn away her guilt, along with her excess adrenaline. Because if he'd died, then…

No. She would not think about that. Unacceptable.

Carlos was fine. Still watching her from the beach. He wasn't going anywhere.

Is he?

Isabella paddled harder now, ripping it up every single time. In the zone at last, she savored the weightless, surreal, nothing-can-touch-me existence where everything wrong and scary and overwhelming disappeared and all that was left were the good feelings.

Like what she felt for Carlos.

Because regardless of the weird things

coming up from her past or the uncertainty of the future, the baby and their relationship, Isabella wanted to suspend time and just enjoy the moments of pure joy and tenderness and comfort she found with him. The pleasure and the understanding, before they disappeared under the stress of daily life and the realities of the things they would have to face soon enough. Custody. Caretaking. Co-parenting.

She took one more long, bumpy, fast-as-hell drop of a wave and rode it all the way in to the shore, finally walking out of the water to the applause of several tourists nearby. She even stopped and posed with her board for them to snap some pictures before joining Carlos on their beach towels, jamming the end of her board into the sand nearby so it stood upright to dry. Her long, loose hair dripped wet, and she squeezed out some of the excess water before plopping down beside him on the towel.

"Did you have fun, *hermosa*?" he asked, his hand warm on her knee through the black wet suit.

"Si."

They sat there in silence a moment or two, staring out at the crushing waves, several other surfers still out there in line. Even a young boy, seven, maybe eight, beside his father, heading out there, his boogie board Velcroed to his wrist with a band. Isabella had started surfing around the same age, going out with her father before her mother had died and Dad had gotten sick.

"You looked at home out there," Carlos said, his voice quiet now, his expression contemplative.

"I love it," she said, wrapping her arms around her knees. "When I'm on a wave, time ceases to exist, and I'm in this intense state of euphoria, peace and excitement." She took a deep breath. "And when I don't have to worry about patients or work or anyone or anything else but me, it's like bliss. I can mess around with my technique and put toes on the nose if I feel like it."

Carlos nodded, sighed. "Sounds magical."

"It is." Isabella shifted slightly to look at him over her shoulder. This morning had been amazing, in no small part due to the man beside her. The fact that she'd nearly lost him only made her want to be near him more. "Almost as good as being with you." She leaned in and kissed him, then rested her forehead against his, eyes closed as guilt choked her throat. "I'm sorry about what happened to you, *cariño.* I never meant for you to get hurt. I should've been more careful with your training. My fault and—"

"Shh." Carlos cupped the back of her head, keeping her close when she started to pull away. "It's okay. I'm okay. Nothing that happened there was your fault. I got distracted and I didn't follow your instructions." He took a deep breath, then exhaled, stirring the hairs around her face, making her shiver. "You are very sexy in your wet suit."

Isabella sat back slightly to look at him, gaze narrowed. Not what she'd been expecting him to say. "What?"

He smiled brighter than the sun coming out from behind a cloud, lighting her world. Everything faded away but the warmth in his gaze. She didn't deserve his kindness, didn't deserve him, but in that moment, as every second they'd spent together so far flashed through her mind, Isabella knew that she didn't just like Carlos. She loved him. And that was probably the worst and most wonderful thing of all.

Confused and concerned, she sat back then, pulling away from him slightly. She needed to gather her thoughts, process all the stuff happening inside her. He let her go, as if sensing she needed space.

"I got really nervous watching you," he said after clearing his throat again. "Those waves are gigantic. Were you scared out there?"

"No. Not even a little." Her father's motto had always been *No fear or go home*. "Fear is dangerous out on the water," she said. "As you learned. I've been shaken a time or two, but I put it behind me quickly and keep going."

It's the same with you.

She kept that last part to herself, realizing it was true. Letting him in had made her feel much the same rush she did surfing—off-kilter, off balance, but connected.

"Well, that's good." Carlos seemed to consider that a moment. "I guess you've surfed even bigger waves?"

"*Si.*" She reached over to trace her finger down his cheek. "You've got a couple more freckles than you had before."

"Do I?" He scrubbed a hand over his jaw as his cheeks reddened slightly.

"*Si.* I think the Barcelona sunshine likes you."

"I like it, too."

She took his hand in hers, entwining their

fingers. "The weather reports said we could get rain later."

"Is that very common?" He brought her hand to his mouth and kissed it. "Rain this time of year?"

Isabella's attention stayed fixed on his mouth, those generous lips, remembering where else he could kiss her, lick her, bring her to ecstasy over and over…

Just then, the little boy and his father came running out of the waves, laughing. They were both drenched but obviously so happy. Her heart pinched a little, remembering her own father in the last days, bedridden and unable to take care of himself. She'd resented him then. Loved him, mourned him and resented him. That old guilt threatened to rob her of breath now.

"Hey," Carlos said, leaning in to kiss her temple. "You okay?"

She nodded, not trusting her voice just then. She wasn't, really. But she would be. Had to be.

"You're amazing, *hermosa*. You know that? Amazing and all good."

"I'm not all good." She frowned, her chest squeezing tighter. "The longer you're around me, you'll find out. Like my siblings. They all couldn't get away from me fast enough."

"I don't believe that." He kissed down her cheek to her jaw, then lower to nuzzle her neck. "I want to stay beside you."

"*Hola,*" a female voice said just then from behind them.

Isabella looked over to see two bikini-clad young women flash their brightest smiles at Carlos, and an unexpected wave of possessiveness dug its claws into her chest, which only freaked her out more. She didn't get jealous. They weren't a couple. They were just two people having a good time together.

And a baby.

Oh, God.

Carlos, for his part, didn't bat an eye. Just shrugged a little, his gaze never leaving Isabella as he said in return, "Hey there."

His dark eyes held so much real, authentic emotion tangled up there, and Isabella had to look away. Too much. It would never be enough. She didn't want any of this, but it was all right there for her, and she didn't know what to do. Her hand trembled in his, and she leaned her head on his shoulder, taking a deep breath to hold it together. God. This wasn't her. Raw and vulnerable and flayed open. She'd been there before when her parents died and had sworn never to go there again. But being with Carlos terrified her.

As if calming a startled colt, he cupped her cheek and smoothed his thumb across her chin. "I only have eyes for you, *hermosa*."

And even that made her afraid. Did she want to be his one and only? Part of her said yes. The other part wasn't sure. Being exclusive, being committed, meant sticking it out no matter what, through sickness and health, till death.

Her heart lodged somewhere near her throat, and when exactly had the temperature risen so much?

Then Carlos threw back his head and laughed harder than she'd ever seen him do before, and suddenly the chains around her snapped. He always surprised her. He probably always would.

"What?" she asked, confused.

"If you could see your face right now, *hermosa*." He shook his head, then met her gaze once more, eyes bright with humor. "Don't worry. I'm not going to ask you to marry me. Not today, anyway."

She sputtered. Had she been that obvious? "I didn't think you would."

He squinted at her. "Yes, I think you did."

Carlos traced a finger down her neck and across her collarbone. Goose bumps popped up on her skin, but she still couldn't quite believe him. No one praised her awesomeness. People just took her for granted. Always had. Then he pulled her into his arms, and she relaxed against him despite her wishes. He made it so easy. Too easy. Her pulse thumped wildly in her chest.

"Let's do something," he said, whispering the words into her hair. "You gave me a peek into your life. Let me do the same for you."

She looked up at him, her brows knit. "Like what? We've been to your uncle's bar already and toured the entire city, visiting all the places in your mother's diary."

"I've got something special in mind," he said, smiling down at her. "A place from the diary I've not shown you yet."

"Really?" She turned slightly to face him, his arms still looped around her middle.

"Really." Carlos grinned now, wide and intoxicating. She totally got why women swooned over him wherever they went. "Tonight. Be ready at seven. Wear something you can move in."

"That's it? That's all you're giving me?"

Isabella shook her head as he laughed. "You know I don't like surprises."

"I know, *hermosa*." He pulled her in and kissed her soundly, then stood, holding out a hand to her. "But for now, you're just going to have to trust me. You can't always be in control."

Isabella blinked up at him, then finally took his hand and allowed him to pull her up. It wasn't that she always had to be in control. She bent to pick up their towels and shake the sand out of them. Okay. Fine. Yes. She liked being in control. But that came from years of *having* to be in control. As for the trust thing… Well, she was working on it.

She rolled up the towels and tucked one under her arm, then handed the other to Carlos to do the same. Then they each grabbed a board to head back to her place. Isabella curled her toes in the warm sand. "Fine. Have it your way. I'll be ready at seven."

CHAPTER EIGHT

AT EIGHT FIFTEEN that night, Isabella and Carlos stood in front of a nondescript gray stone building on a side street in Sant Marti. The sounds of a busy street nearby echoed around them, and the air smelled of fried food from the street vendors and the rain from a couple hours before. Not exactly the lovely romantic fantasy she'd had in mind. She scrunched her nose and looked up at him. "This is it?"

"This is it." He winked at her, then opened the door, leading her up a narrow set of steps inside.

"And your parents came here?" she asked, staring at his back in front of her, her hand in his, tugging her forward.

"They did." Carlos looked back over his shoulder at her through the shadows. Dim sconces on the walls cast yellow light and shadows everywhere. He waggled his brows at her. "It's where my mother taught my father the dance of love."

Isabella gave him a suspicious look. "Where exactly did you bring me?" Even having lived in the city her whole life, she wasn't familiar with this address. "It's not illegal, is it?"

"No, *hermosa*. Not illegal." He snorted. "Just relax and enjoy. It will be fun."

Great. Isabella really wasn't a "just relax and enjoy" kind of person, but she'd go along with it since Carlos seemed so excited to show her this place.

They stopped at the top of the stairs, and she squinted at the wall where a line of black-and-white photos hung. Couples dressed in clothing from the '50s and '60s, dancing and laughing and embracing, all smiling and looking carefree. Huh. All the people were more formally dressed than the pink top and skirt she'd worn. Maybe she should've chosen something else. Her pulse quickened and her chest squeezed. Maybe this was a mistake after all.

"Hey." Carlos stood behind her, his hands on her hips, his warmth melting the thin line of ice traveling down her spine. "Do you trust me, *hermosa*?"

She nodded, swallowing hard. She tried. Really, really tried.

"*Buena,*" he said, and she studied his reflection in the glass of one of the photos. Gorgeous, as always. Tall, lean and powerful. His dark, curly hair was loose tonight, not tamed as it usually was for work. After all the sun earlier, he looked tanned and freer now, younger and more approachable. His long-sleeved gray shirt drew her gaze to the muscled lines of his chest and taut abs. Around his neck, in the hollow of his throat, dangled the small silver cross that he'd told her had belonged to his mother.

By the time she glanced back up at his face, his bemused expression slowly transformed into a smile. "Come. Let's go inside."

At the end of the hall, they stopped at a door. There were no numbers or signs to give her a hint of what she might see on the other side. Carlos winked at her once more, opened the door and flipped on the lights.

A high ceiling soared above them, covered in beautiful, warm oak, and mirrors surrounded them on three sides. The floor itself was bigger than her whole flat, and a small stage sat at one end, filled with stereo equipment. Isabella gaped at it all. She couldn't have been more stunned if he'd presented her with a live elephant. "What is this place?"

Carlos grinned and closed the door behind them. "A dance studio. It belongs to a friend of mine from Cuba. You like it?"

"*Si.* It's beautiful." She followed him down to the small stage, where he started turning on the stereo equipment. "But where is everyone?"

"The studio is closed tonight." He put on a slow, instrumental piece full of soaring, sweet melodies and a singer lamenting love and heartbreak in Spanish. "It's just for us."

"Oh," she said, letting that sink in. "Oh!"

"*Si.*" He began to move with the rhythm, stepping and rotating his hips and oh! He was good at that. He held out a hand to her, but she shied away. Isabella had never had time for dancing when she was growing up and figured it was probably too late to learn now. Carlos gave her a look, then smiled slow, those dimples of his beckoning her to him. "Come, *hermosa*. Don't worry. I'll teach you."

The music changed then, and the air filled with the quick, throbbing, syncopated beats of a samba, the kind of music the clubs down by the beach played. The clubs Isabella didn't usually have time to go to because of work.

She'd always liked that kind of music, though, and found her toes tapping despite herself.

Carlos waggled his fingers at her. "Come on. I let you teach me surfing. Let me teach you dancing. I love it. It's been a part of me since I can remember. Dancing is like life in Cuba. Everyone does it everywhere." He did a little turn on his heels and ended facing her again with a grin. "Trust me?"

She wanted to. She really wanted to. Fingers trembling, she reached for him.

His fingers tightened around hers, and he led her to the middle of the huge floor, then took her into his arms, his hand on her lower back and their bodies close. As if sensing her wariness, he leaned down and whispered in her ear, "Don't be nervous, *hermosa*. It's just dancing. You can't drown here."

That made her gasp and smack him. "I told you I never meant for that to happen. I'm so sorry about—"

He laughed out loud then, placing a finger over her lips to silence her. "A joke, *hermosa*. But it worked. You are not so nervous now, eh?"

She opened her mouth to argue, but he was right. Then he stroked his fingers up and down her spine, and a new kind of tension build within her that had nothing to do with nerves and everything to do with wanting the man holding her. "I might not be any good at this, you know. Best watch your toes."

"I think you will be amazing at it. Watching you surf, I already know you have superb muscle memory and grace. You just need to learn the right steps. Those I can teach you."

His crooked grin and warm gaze eased her concerns and Isabella nodded, closing her eyes and allowing the musical rhythm pounding in her chest to take over her body. Carlos's strong, solid grip made her feel safe. She peeked one eye open and glanced up at him through her lashes and saw him smiling, a spark of amusement in his dark eyes. "Ready?"

"Yes."

"*Buena.*" He used his body to lead her back a step, then forward. They did that a few times until she loosened up and stopped hesitating over each move. Then he let his arm slip away from her back and raised the other, and she did a little spin without thinking about it.

Once her brain kicked in again, Isabella froze and gasped. "Was that right?"

"*Si.*" He put his hands on her shoulders and massaged them lightly. "There is no right or wrong here with us. Just do what you feel. It's all good."

They started again. Backward, forward, spin. Backward, forward, spin.

He chuckled. "Feels better, eh?"

"How did you know?"

"Dancing is in my blood," he said, then winked. "And your body is relaxed against mine."

The music switched again, this time to something faster and lighter. An older song she'd heard on the radio many times growing up and loved, by a popular Latina singer in America. Carlos grinned and spun her around again before taking her into his arms once more. "Let's get loud, eh?"

"*Si.* I love this song!"

As the music played on and they danced more, Isabella forgot all about her nerves. She forgot all about her cares and worries and the stresses of the past and her job and just lived in the moment with Carlos. If his parents had done this during their whirlwind romance, she could understand why Carlos's father had fallen under his mother's spell. Dancing like this felt magical, freeing, fantastic. She'd never thought she'd feel the same emotions she did when surfing anywhere else, but here she did, and she had Carlos to thank. He'd given her this, and she felt so grateful.

Then she stepped forward when she should have stepped back and crushed his toes.

"Oh, God!" She covered her mouth with her hands. "I'm so sorry. Are you okay?"

"I'm fine, *hermosa*." He winced slightly and shook out his foot. "I've been stepped on much worse than that many times before. You should see the salsa clubs in Havana on a Saturday night. So packed you barely have any room to move in there. I've suffered broken toes and all. You just keep dancing."

He coaxed her back into his arms again, though she felt stiffer than ever now. First the riptide, and now she'd stomped on his foot. She was hopeless.

"Relax, *hermosa*." He ducked slightly to catch her eye, then held her gaze. "Look at me, yes? Just keep looking at me. Feel me. Then we will be fine. You'll see."

She did, stumbling slightly again, but he never let her fall. Then she got distracted by his soft, full lips and the memory of how they felt on hers. The music changed to a slow, beautiful piece once more, this time with a bit of melancholy in the melody. Carlos pulled her closer, leading her so naturally, just as he did in life. Responsive, strong, never pushy or overbearing—and she finally let go again. Closed her eyes and was just there, with him in that moment, and the rest of the world fell away.

At least until Carlos whispered into her ear, "Do you love me?"

Isabella froze, blinking at him, her gums throbbing with her pulse. "What?"

"I asked if you love the rumba," he said, looking at her strangely. "It's my favorite dance. Why? What did you think I said?"

"Oh…um…" The music had stopped now, leaving only the sounds of their breathing and the echoes from the world outside. She shook her head and looked away, face hot. "I'm not sure. And yes, the rumba is very nice." Her throat felt dry and scratchy, and she suddenly needed air. Fresh air. She backed away slowly toward the door. "I'm going to step outside for a moment. Get something to drink."

Carlos stood there, watching her, his dark eyes unreadable for once, as she fled the dance studio like a coward. Because yes. She did love him. Against all her wishes and better judgment, and now she had no idea what to do about that.

* * *

Carlos waited for a while inside the studio, shutting off the music and leaving a note for his friend, thanking them for letting him use their place. He still wasn't quite sure exactly what he'd done to scare off Isabella like that, but she'd been spooked.

Each time he closed his eyes, he saw her pale face, her wide eyes, the way she'd shied away from him like a wounded animal. So very different from how soft and free and wonderful she'd been in his arms. She'd been a great dancer, just as he'd imagined, when she let herself relax.

He sighed and shut off the lights, then closed and locked the door. He shouldn't have mentioned love. That was the problem. In his experience, love always meant loss or pain. And while he tried to face life with an open heart, it was still hard, and he remained guarded about many things.

Not about Isabella, though. Try as he might to fight it, to not open his heart to her too soon, she'd managed to get in anyway. Sweet and funny and kind and smart and wonderful and beautiful. There was no way for him to resist her combination. Isabella was everything he'd ever wanted in a partner and more. So much more. She'd somehow broken down his carefully constructed walls without him even knowing, and now, suddenly, he couldn't imagine his life without her. Didn't want to. No matter what fears she might have, he knew deep down that he loved her.

The truth of it vibrated through his bones like a tuning fork, solidifying like steel, making him both stronger and more vulnerable at the same time. *I love Isabella Rivas.* And now that the words were out there—in his head and his heart, anyway—there was no going back. He wouldn't tell her yet, though, especially after what had just happened in the dance studio. He'd seen the wariness in her eyes, the fear. Had felt the same himself in the past. But now he knew. And he loved her all the same. Deep and strong and alive. Scary, too, such a new realization, but exciting. Like a tiny bird that would grow into a giant.

But for now, he would keep it to himself. Get used to the idea. Perhaps think of a way to tell Isabella that wouldn't spook her or make her feel like he was trying to put chains on her or control her. Only that he loved her and wanted to be with her and their baby, however she would let him.

Si. Keeping it inside for now would work better.

After checking the hallway and not seeing her there, he jogged downstairs and went outside once more. He found Isabella leaning against the side of the building, staring down at her toes, looking sad. His first instinct was to comfort her, to wrap his arms around her and hold her close until she smiled again. But her earlier wariness made him cautious. So, instead, he just walked over and leaned against the wall beside her, not saying a word.

After a minute or two, she finally looked over at him beneath the orangish glow of the streetlight nearby. "I'm sorry for ruining things upstairs."

"You didn't ruin anything, *hermosa*. I just wish you could talk to me about what's bothering you."

"I…" She huffed out a breath, then stared at the quiet street in front of them. "I don't know. I misheard you upstairs, and it just… I don't know."

"Ah," he said, hiding his wince. So, it had been the *L* word. His chest ached knowing that she wasn't in the same place as him, but hopefully with more time, she would get there. Isabella's walls were built high and mighty, but Carlos was not a man who gave up on what he wanted easily. Still, they had time. Eager to move on to something less heavy and get her comfortable and smiling again, he tried humor. "So, you hated my rumba, then?"

"What?" She gave him a surprised stare. "No. The dancing was amazing. Seriously. I had no idea you could move that way."

He grinned, leaning his head back against the cool gray stone to stare up at the stars. "Like I said, everyone dances in Havana. I learned when I was four, I think, from my grandfather. He used to take me with him to the square in our neighborhood for the evening fiestas. Everyone gathered there. A little party every night. Food and drinks and music, to help people unwind. We didn't have much, but we had each other. Once the band started to play, they'd clear the tables away and people would dance. By themselves, together, didn't matter. All good fun."

"Sounds like it," Isabella said, mirroring his position. Always a good sign. She sighed and closed her eyes, her beautiful face lifted skyward. "The most we ever did in my house was game night. We'd play checkers or board games or whatever, once my younger siblings were old enough to be on teams. Someone always got mad, though, because they didn't win, or because they thought someone else was cheating." She laughed. "My dad even played sometimes. At least until his MS got too bad and kept him in bed all the time."

Her smile fell then, and Carlos would've given his whole world to bring it back. Impossible, he knew, but maybe they could try something else instead. "Gelato."

"I'm sorry?" Isabella looked over at him.

"I'm in the mood for gelato."

"For dinner?"

"*Si.*" He straightened and held out his hand to her, living and dying in those few seconds until she took it, her skin warm and soft against him. "For dinner. Unless you have something else you prefer?"

She tucked herself into his side, holding on to his arm and resting her head against the side of his shoulder as they walked away from the dance studio. "No. Gelato sounds perfect to me."

Not exactly the ending to the evening he'd imagined, and there were still many things—important things—they needed to discuss, but they could wait. For now, things were back to normal, and he was glad.

CHAPTER NINE

THE NEXT COUPLE of days flew by in a haze for Isabella. She felt happier and freer than she had in a long time, maybe ever, and the last thing she wanted to do was trigger her old issues when things were going so well with Carlos.

She really, really liked him. Isabella wasn't ready to go beyond that yet, because...well. They were still getting to know each other, and things were good between them. Very, very good. And no one fell in love that quickly, right? No. That was silly. Besides, Isabella didn't do love. Love meant obligations and responsibilities, and this thing with Carlos was all about exploration and freedom and...

"Hey, you in there?" Mario said from the driver's seat.

Isabella blinked over at him, realizing that

she'd zoned out again, lost in her head. It had been happening a lot lately, and she couldn't blame it all on the pregnancy hormones, either. Nope. One more reason not to get carried away with Carlos. Too distracting. Even if the sex blew her mind and shook her world and…

The two-way radio in the ambulance crackled to life with a new call from the dispatcher. "Units respond to a motor vehicle accident in the tunnel on Plaça d'Espanya. Vehicle has rolled over onto the roof. Driver trapped inside. Fire department is on scene already, waiting for paramedic assist."

"On our way," Mario answered in Catalan, then signaled to change lanes and head in that direction.

Unfortunately, it wasn't the first rollover they'd had in that area. People tended to drive too fast through there, and accidents happened. The problem with rollovers was, you never knew how badly the people inside were hurt until you got them out of the vehicle.

While Mario navigated through the early-evening traffic, Isabella went into the back of the rig to get everything ready for them once they arrived—she checked and stocked the medical kits and got their hard hats and heavy gear ready in case they had to get into the wrecked vehicle to help stabilize a patient. Cases like this were tough anyway, and the fact that she was pregnant would make it even harder, but she still hadn't told anyone yet, other than Carlos, and Isabella wanted to keep it that way if possible.

A few minutes later, they pulled up to the scene and found two lanes of traffic cordoned off by police, who were rerouting cars around the accident site. The vehicle lay on its top, one side resting against the stone wall of the tunnel. Shattered glass from the windshield sparkled on the black asphalt beneath the yellow lights above. The air smelled of burned rubber and exhaust. Isabella climbed out of the rig and headed over to a firefighter standing nearby.

"How many people are trapped inside?" Isabella asked him.

"Just one, as far as we can tell," the burly man said. "We'll hold the car steady if you want to check on the driver."

Isabella nodded, then headed toward the shattered driver's side window to crouch next to it, glancing up at the firefighters holding the car in place. "Make sure this thing doesn't flip over on me, okay!"

The fire crew chuckled and nodded. Isabella grinned back, then focused on the driver, calling out to Mario, who stood nearby. She was smaller and therefore better able to maneuver in the close quarters of the damaged car, they'd agreed. "He's alive and conscious. Tangled up in his seat belt. Sir, can you move your legs?"

The victim shook his head. "Caught on something."

"Okay. Sir, sit very still while the fire department removes this door for you. It will be loud for a moment, but don't worry. We're right here and won't let anything happen to you."

He nodded, and Isabella moved back to allow another firefighter in with the jaws of life to cut off the car door, which had been badly damaged in the accident. Once the area was cleared again and they'd stabilized the car, Isabella got back down on the ground to crawl inside the vehicle to better examine the patient. Pulse good, blood pressure slightly elevated, but not concerning given the circumstances. And the man seemed to be conscious and alert. The one thing that struck her as odd, though, were golf clubs scattered everywhere.

"Are you a golfer, sir?"

"I am," he said in American English. "On vacation with my wife. She's back at the hotel while I went out to shoot a round or two at Can Cuyàs. On my way back to our hotel when this happened. I love golf."

A strong smell of alcohol clung to the man's breath, and Isabella wondered exactly how much drinking had occurred with his golfing. She was about to ask when a loud screeching noise issued from the metal frame of the car and the whole thing tipped forward, onto the hood. The firefighters shouted and golf clubs went flying around the interior of the car. Isabella turned to shield the patient, still tangled in his seat belt, when something heavy struck the side of her head and her vision tunneled. The last thing she remembered was the shouts of the firefighters and Mario's voice, echoing from far, far away.

"Isabella! Isabella? Get them out of there now!"

"Isabella! Isabella?" Carlos stared down into her pale face, his throat constricted. When the call had come in that they were bringing in a rollover accident, Carlos had prepped to receive the incoming patient with the rest of the ER staff. But then they'd brought in not one, but two gurneys, and his stomach had dropped. Even more so when Mario rushed in beside the second gurney, shaken and gray.

Carlos had made a beeline straight for Isabella's partner, knowing he had to excuse himself from the case because he and Isabella were involved but wanting to be by her side anyway. His mind whirled as he listened to Mario tell the doctor what happened. "We were on scene," the paramedic said. "The fire department had a hold of the vehicle. Isabella crawled inside to check the victim, and the car slipped. Something struck her in the head, and she lost consciousness."

Dr. Gonçalo checked Isabella's eyes. "Pupils even and reactive."

Good. That was good. Carlos tried to keep focused on the work, on doing what he was trained to do, but he couldn't. This wasn't just another patient. This was Isabella. The woman carrying his child. The woman he…

"Martinez?" Dr. Gonçalo called to him, breaking Carlos out of his thought bubble. "You okay?"

"Uh…" He stared down at Isabella's still form, her pale face, the already darkening bruise on her forehead and the shallow cut above her eyebrow, blood bright red against her too-white skin. Slowly, Carlos stepped back, trembling hands held up before him, palms out. "I…uh. No. I'm sorry. I can't do this. I can't treat this case. Isabella and I… We're…" Another step back. This wasn't how he wanted the world to find out they were a couple, but it couldn't be helped. "We're seeing each other."

A hush fell over the team as every eye in the room turned toward him. Only the beep of the monitors and the distant bustle of the ER outside their trauma space echoed around him. Then, just as quickly as the silence had started, it ended, and reality snapped back into place.

"Fine. Nurse Ramirez, please get CT scans and skull X-rays," Dr. Gonçalo ordered. "Once we have the results, we'll go from there." She leaned over Isabella again and patted her cheek. "Ms. Rivas? Isabella? Can you hear me? Squeeze my fingers if you can hear me."

Nothing.

"Isabella?" Dr. Gonçalo called, a bit more forcefully this time. "Can you wake up for me? Isabella?"

She stirred a bit on the table then, scowling, her eyes darting behind closed lids as she mumbled something indecipherable, except for the last two words—"...the baby."

Dr. Gonçalo frowned and looked over at Mario again. "Was there a baby involved in the accident, too?"

"No." Mario shook his head. "Only the one man behind the wheel. He's in the next trauma room."

"Then what's she talking about?" Dr. Gonçalo asked, her attention transferring to Carlos.

Heat prickled up his neck from beneath the collar of his scrub shirt. He swallowed hard past the tension constricting his throat. *Tell them. They need to know.* He blurted out the truth in a nervous rush. "She's pregnant. Isabella's pregnant. It's mine. She's just over two months along."

"What the—?" another male voice said. Carlos whirled around to find Diego Rivas, a neonatal surgeon at St. Aelina's and Isabella's younger brother, behind him. Diego grabbed Carlos by the arm and hauled him into the hallway, crowding him up against the wall with his body, his expression hard as steel. "Explain to me what you just said."

This wasn't going well. Not at all.

Carlos took a deep breath through his nose,

his hot back pressed to the cool wall behind him, sweat itching on the nape of his neck. Part of him wanted to shove past Dr. Rivas and get back in there with Isabella, but the other part of him knew he wasn't going anywhere until they had this out.

He exhaled slow then nodded. "Your sister and I have been seeing each other for a few weeks."

"A few weeks?" One of Diego's dark brows rose. "Two months is more than a few weeks."

Wow. Okay. His stomach dropped from where it was crowding his chest to somewhere near his toes. He'd known Isabella hadn't wanted to tell her coworkers about the pregnancy because she didn't want rumors started, but he'd assumed she'd at least told her family. The fact she hadn't gave him a sour taste in his mouth. He blinked back into a pair of dark eyes nearly identical to Isabella's and said, "We had a very brief affair back in April. We were careful then, but…"

"Not careful enough, apparently." Diego squared his shoulders and crossed his arms, easing away a few inches, but not enough to let Carlos escape. The man stood a good five inches taller than Isabella and looked like solid muscle. Carlos kept in shape, too, but he really didn't want to get into it with her brother, especially right now. He wanted to get back in there and make sure she was okay. He sidled out from where he stood, but Diego stopped him, jaw tight. "What's happened to my sister?"

"A concussion," Carlos said. "They were working at a vehicle accident scene, and she struck her head. That's all I know so far."

After a flat stare that seemed to last a small eternity, Diego stepped back, allowing Carlos to relax a bit. His shoulders stiffened and his chest tingled. Uncomfortable and filled with foreboding, he sidestepped back toward the trauma room, where the radiology techs had arrived to take Isabella for her tests. "I, uh, I should get back in there."

Diego watched him, his expression unreadable. "We'll talk more about this later."

Carlos had no doubt. But as he walked beside Isabella's gurney toward the elevators, holding her hand, he couldn't help thinking all this secrecy about the baby couldn't be good for their future together. Hell, he knew better than anyone what lies and hidden truths could do to a family, and he never wanted a child of his to suffer what he had. Isabella kept everyone at arm's length, including him and her family. And while he cared for her a great deal—more than a great deal, honestly—this would never work if they couldn't be truthful with each other and with everyone else about what was happening and what they meant to each other.

They rode up to the radiology department, and Carlos watched from nearby as they did the head X-rays and CT scan, taking extra precautions due to the pregnancy. It wasn't until they were finished, and Carlos stood by her side again, that Isabella regained consciousness. She blinked open her eyes, squinting up at the ceiling and the bright lights.

"Wh-what's happening?" Her voice sounded thready and weak, making his heart clench tight. "Wh-where am I?"

Carlos kissed her hand, then smiled down at her, pulling up a chair to her bedside. "You're at St. Aelina's, *hermosa*. You were hurt during the accident. Do you remember anything about that?"

She frowned. "I remember being in the vehicle with the patient, examining him, then a loud noise, and everything tilted. My head hurts really bad."

"*Si.*" Carlos gave her a small smile, then kissed the back of her hand again, holding it close to his chest. "The firefighters lost their grip on the car. It slipped and Mario said a golf club smacked you in the head."

Isabella gave a tiny snort. "I knew there was a reason I never liked that sport." Then she sobered, her eyes widening. "The baby. Is the baby okay?"

"The baby's fine," Carlos reassured her. "Hopefully, these scans will be clear and you'll only have a nasty bump and a bruise for a while."

He tried to keep his rising sadness and distress over the situation with her family under wraps, but apparently not as well as he'd wanted, because she narrowed her gaze.

"What's wrong?" she asked.

"Nothing, *hermosa*. I'm worried about you, that's all."

"Are you sure?" She looked unconvinced, but then the radiology techs returned to wheel her back down to the ER. Carlos walked along beside her, forcing a smile.

"I'm sure." The fact Isabella didn't try to pull away only showed him how out of it she was. Because if she'd been lucid, she never would've held hands with him within the walls of St. Aelina's. Too many people could see, too many rumors could start. And that made him more confused and sadder than ever.

CHAPTER TEN

"HOW ARE YOU FEELING?" Carlos asked Isabella for what felt like the millionth time. "Anything I can get you?"

She bit back a snarky reply as he leaned her forward to fluff the pillows behind her head, like she was an invalid. Considering that since she'd come to stay at his flat following her release from the ER two days prior—at his insistence—she kind of felt like one. She gave him a bland smile instead. "I'm fine, thanks. You know, I'm perfectly capable of getting up and doing things for myself."

"Nope. Not yet." Carlos sat on the edge of the bed and gave her a stern look. "Dr. Gonçalo said nothing strenuous until she's seen you for a recheck tomorrow."

Being on the receiving end of convalescence wasn't something she was used to, and it rubbed her the wrong way. And while she felt grateful for Carlos being there for her, she couldn't shake the feeling that he was hiding something from her. Something important. She'd gotten the same weird vibes from him in the ER, when he'd seemed unaccountably sad.

Isabella had tried several times to get him to talk to her about what was bothering him, but so far, he hadn't said anything. Well, if she was stuck here with him pampering her to death, she'd get it out of him one way or another. Being standoffish hadn't done it, so maybe some genuine honey would work.

"Hey." She reached over and took his hand. "Thank you for all you've done for me. I appreciate you taking care of me. I know I'm not always the best patient."

He snorted, and she frowned. "You are so not the best patient. That old saying is true, about medical workers making the most awful patients."

"I'm not that bad."

Carlos gave her a flat look.

Isabella huffed out a breath, her shoulders slumping. "Okay, fine. Maybe I am that bad." She sighed and clasped her hands in her lap, leaning back against the headboard, cushioned by her recently fluffed pillows. Her head still ached a bit. Nothing major, though. She had an egg-size lump and a purplish-green bruise near her right temple where the five iron had beaned her good, but otherwise she was fine.

Isabella shook her head, smiling as an old memory resurfaced. "I remember one time, when I was about sixteen, I'd nursed the rest of the family through a bout of flu and then finally came down with it myself. It was awful. And my poor brother Diego had to take care of me. Talk about worst patients ever."

Carlos's warm smile faltered at the mention of her brother.

Isabella, ever observant, picked up on it immediately, and her stomach tightened. Diego working at St. Aelina's was a never-ending source of ugh for her. One of the reasons why she was so careful to stay out of the gossip mill at the hospital, too, because once Diego caught scent of something, he never let it go. She narrowed her gaze on Carlos. "What's wrong?"

"Huh?" He glanced up at her from where he'd been staring at their joined hands as if lost in thought. Carlos gave a quick shake of his head. "Nothing. Why?"

"Because I know you're lying to me."

He scoffed and straightened. "I'm not lying. What in the world would I have to lie about?"

"No idea." She crossed her arms, realizing maybe Diego wasn't the only stubborn Rivas. "But I know there's something. I can tell. You were acting strangely when we were in radiology after my scans. And now again, after I brought up my brother Diego." Isabella pursed her lips. "You might as well tell me, because I won't stop asking until you do."

For a moment, Carlos looked like he'd argue with her about it, but then his stiff posture crumpled, and he exhaled slow. He stared down at their hands again instead of meeting her gaze, his dark brows drawn together. "Why haven't you told your family about the baby yet?"

That knocked her back a bit. "Oh, well. I don't know. At first, like I said, I wanted to make sure it would be a viable pregnancy. Then, later, I guess I just never got around to it. I wanted to find the right time, I suppose."

Carlos nodded, his frown deepening. "Diego knows."

"What?" Eyes wide, she sat forward, the pillows behind her scattering to either side. "How?"

Dots of crimson darkened along Carlos's high cheekbones. "He was there, in the ER, in the hallway when I told Dr. Gonçalo about the pregnancy."

"Wait." She swung her legs over the side of the bed and started to get up, swallowing hard at the wave of dizziness that overtook her. Isabella waited a moment, willing the bile burning her throat to recede before finally pushing to her feet. Carlos didn't stop her this time, which was a good thing, because she wasn't in the mood to be coddled now. She was too pissed off. "So, you're telling me that you specifically went against my wishes and told my brother about us and the baby?"

"What choice did I have?" He stood as well, raking a hand through his hair before taking her arm to steady her when she wobbled. "Please, *hermosa*. Sit down and let's talk about this."

"No." She pulled away from him and stumbled back a step before catching herself with a hand on the wall. "I don't want to sit. I want you to tell me exactly what the hell happened in the ER."

Carlos took a deep breath, then another, his head dropping until he stared at his feet. "When they brought you in alongside the man who'd been trapped in the car, I was as shocked as anyone. I had to excuse myself from the case, of course, because we are together. And when Dr. Gonçalo ordered the X-rays and scans on you, I had to tell them about the baby so they could take proper precautions."

He cursed under his breath, then met her gaze. "Your brother Diego happened to hear about you being brought in and rushed down to the ER to check on you. He was standing behind me when I told all that to Dr. Gonçalo. By then it was too late to take it back, and he pulled me into the hall to ask me about it."

"And you told him."

Not a question.

Isabella backed into a chair in the corner and sank into it, covering her face with her hands. It wasn't that she didn't want her family to know about the baby. They'd find out eventually, obviously. But she'd just wanted a little more time to...adjust herself first. To wrap her head around the fact that in less than seven months, she'd have a baby of her own, a little boy or girl to take care of, to love and cherish forever. But also a child she'd have to care for, support, worry about every minute of every day. What if they were sick? What if they were born with a disability? What if she was a horrible mother? *Gah!* She'd just wanted more time to come to grips with all her fears and foibles before springing the shock on her family. And then, of course, because she knew her siblings so well, she knew they'd all want to fawn over her, take care of her. And the last thing she wanted or needed right now was more coddling.

"Look," Carlos said, crouching beside her chair but not touching her. "I'm sorry that things happened the way they did, but I'm not sorry people know, *hermosa*. After how I grew up, after what happened with my parents, there's one thing I know. Happiness is fleeting and you must grab it where you can. I've found happiness, here with you and the baby. I understand things with you and your family are complicated, after your mother's death and you having to grow up and be responsible for everyone so young. But this is our future we're talking about, Isabella. Our baby."

"My future," she said, defensiveness flaring hot inside her, burning through her common sense. She loved Carlos, but her old fears and pain clouded her vision, made her shrink away. "My baby."

He blinked at her, raw pain and confusion in his dark eyes. "*Hermosa?* What are you saying?"

"I'm saying that you're getting too far ahead of yourself here, Carlos." She shook her head, holding herself tighter around her middle, like a shield against the things that were too scary and too intense to feel with him—for him. She pushed to unsteady feet, glad for the chair behind her to catch her, but needing to get this out now, before she couldn't anymore. It felt like she was thirteen again and the walls were closing in around her, leaving only one path ahead for her to follow, suffocating her with rules and responsibilities and a single choice for the future. She couldn't breathe, couldn't move, couldn't do anything except fight back. "There is no us. Not yet. Maybe not ever. We made a baby together, that's it. It's not a lifetime commitment. For you. I can do this by myself if I have to."

"No!" He straightened, towering over her, becoming angry for the first time since she'd known him, eyes bright and cheeks flushed. "This is my baby, too. I will not let my child grow up the way I did. Not knowing who they are. Not knowing who they come from. I will not do it, Isabella!"

"And I won't ever allow myself to be caged in again, Carlos. Not by you. Not by anyone. I love you, but I can't do this. I'm not ready yet. Maybe someday I will be, but not now. Not yet. I'm sorry."

They stared at each other across the span of a few feet, Isabella's cheeks wet with tears and the color slowly draining from Carlos's tanned face. The air around them chilled, and Isabella shivered with the finality of it all. Her heart ached and her chest squeezed tight. She loved Carlos. She did. But she wasn't ready to settle down and make a life with him.

It was obvious from the way his lips tightened and his breath hitched that he was ready to move forward with her. Or had been. Until she'd thrown it all back in his face. Voice edged in ice, he turned away, heading for the door, only to stop on the threshold and look back at her to say. "I see, Isabella. My mistake. I thought we wanted the same things here, but apparently not. Excuse me."

Isabella stood there after he walked out of the room, feeling more alone and desolate than she ever had in her life. She missed him already, but she had to carry on—for herself and for her baby.

* * *

"What did I do wrong, *Tío*?" Carlos asked later that night. He'd gone downstairs to Encanteri after Isabella had moved back to her own flat earlier—against his wishes. Their last discussion had not ended well, but dammit. The fact that she'd kept the pregnancy a secret from everyone, even those closest to her, triggered all his old doubts and fears. Now, as he sat there, nursing a beer that had grown warm over the past hour or so, his skin felt too tight and all his joints too loose. Discombobulated. A word he'd read once, and it seemed to fit, even though he wasn't totally clear on its meaning.

Uncle Hugo raised a bushy gray brow at him, then sighed. "It's nothing you've done, *sobrino*." He shook his head and frowned down at the glass he polished. For once, things were slower at the bar that night, so they could talk and hear one another. Even the music on the overhead speakers sounded slow and melancholy. Figured. "Sometimes, the heart wants what it wants."

Carlos dropped his head into his hands and groaned, sudden anger surging inside him. "Bullshit."

"Excuse me?" Hugo put the glass down and narrowed his gaze on his nephew.

"The heart wants what it wants," Carlos scoffed, hands flying now as he spoke. Heat prickled the back of his neck as people nearby turned to stare at him, but he didn't care. His heart hurt, and he'd kept a cap on his emotions too long, trying to earn Isabella's trust and love. Now she'd thrown it all back in his face, then stomped on his love on top of it all. No. No more. He was done. "That's a lie, *Tío*. Because all I ever wanted was to be with Isabella, and she's gone and..."

He managed to cut himself off before mentioning the baby—barely. And it didn't matter that he hadn't told anyone yet, either—well, except for the entire ER at St. Aelina's—because he had just been trying to obey Isabella's wishes.

Hugo inhaled deep, then exhaled slowly through his nose, as summoning all his patience. "Your father."

Carlos waited for him to continue, staring down at the dark wood bar top. When he didn't, Carlos finally looked up at his uncle. The sore spot in his chest that had been there pretty much his entire life where his dad was concerned pinched harder. He was thirty-four.

He shouldn't care about his father anymore. The man who hadn't loved him enough to even try to find him after Carlos was born. It shouldn't matter. It still did. With more bitterness than he'd intended, Carlos said, "What about him?"

"I've never told you about how he was after your mother left," Hugo said, watching him closely. "You remind me of him, *sobrino.* Same impulsiveness, recklessness, always leading with your heart and not your head."

"I am not reckless!" The few patrons in the bar went silent, and Carlos realized he'd said that way louder than he'd meant to. Dammit. He slumped down on his stool and tried to make himself smaller to avoid the unwanted attention. "I'm not reckless," he repeated, quieter this time. "Or impulsive. If anything, I've tried my hardest to never be that way. The last thing I want to end up as is my father."

Then he winced. Uncle Hugo was the sweetest man Carlos had ever known. Generous, kind, compassionate. In fact, there'd been times he'd wished that Hugo had been his father. But he'd always been cognizant of the fact that Hugo had been his father, Alejandro's, brother. He'd never been too harsh in his criticisms to avoid hurting Hugo. But tonight, all his defenses had been trampled, and he had nothing left. Still, he hated the stricken look on his uncle's face, no matter how fast he'd hidden it behind his usual easygoing smile. Carlos hung his head and squeezed his eyes shut. "I'm sorry, *Tío*. I didn't mean..."

"You did." Hugo cleared his throat and put the glass away behind him before leaning his hands on the edge of the bar, leaning closer to Carlos. "And you're right."

Carlos looked up again, confused. "About what?"

"About everything." Hugo sighed and came around the bar to take a seat on the stool beside Carlos's. "Look, I can't imagine what you and your mother must've gone through back in Cuba." When Carlos opened his mouth, Hugo held up a hand to stop him. "I know. I know that we've talked about a lot of things, but I also know that you've held a lot back from me, trying to protect my feelings, because that's who you are, *sobrino*." He flashed a sad little smile. "Such a good man. Better than your father. Better than me, too."

"That's not true. You are a wonderful man," Carlos assured him, his head muddled from too much emotion and too little alcohol. He should've gotten fall-down drunk and fallen asleep upstairs. That would've avoided this embarrassing scene in the bar and the raw vulnerability he felt inside. Maybe he'd have slept it off and felt better in the morning. Given the ache in his chest, though, he doubted it. "I'm sorry. I'm upset about Isabella, and I shouldn't have taken it out on you."

"Stop it," his uncle said, in a far harsher tone than Carlos had ever heard him use before. "Stop explaining and denying and excusing what is inexcusable."

"I'm—"

"No. You stop talking and listen to me. I'm going to tell you some things about your father. Things that I have kept back from you as well."

Carlos blinked at Hugo, more than a bit stunned. After the hours and hours he and his uncle had spent talking about the past after Carlos had first arrived in Barcelona, he'd doubted there was anything he didn't know about his father. But apparently, he was wrong.

"The letter. The one your mother wrote to Alejandro telling him that she was pregnant with you," Hugo said, staring down at his hands in his lap, his fingers worrying the edge of the apron he wore. "Your father never received it."

"What?" Carlos frowned, not quite computing that information. "What do you mean?"

"I mean, the letter arrived, but our parents intercepted it before your father had a chance to see it. He never knew about you. Not until after they died."

Jesus. The earth tilted beneath Carlos's feet, and he gripped the bar tight. "I don't even know what to say about that."

Hugo winced. "I know. And I'm sorry. We had no idea, Alejandro and I, that you even existed until they passed away fifteen years ago and I found the letters your mother and her parents had sent." He shook his head. "Even then, I kept it from your father. He still didn't know. I didn't want him to dwell in the past anymore. He'd been stuck there for so long, miserable, with no relief, no end in sight. I just wanted him to find peace and happiness after all those years. I intended to tell him. I swear I did, but then he got sick, and he passed away, and it was too late. I'm so, so sorry, Carlos. About everything."

"But… I…" This was way too much for him to take in. Like everything he'd thought was true wasn't. Lies. All lies. All those years, all that heartache. All those nights lying awake wondering about his father, where he was, who he was, if he missed Carlos like Carlos missed him. None of that happened, because his father had never known he'd existed. The ball of dread inside him sank deeper into a black hole of despair. "Why would you do that, *Tío*? I trusted you. I came here, to you, to learn more about myself, about my past. And you lied to me."

Hugo blanched beneath his tan, the lines on his face more pronounced. Gone was the gregarious bar owner, always cheerful and laughing. In his place was an old man who looked every one of his sixty years. "I never meant to, *sobrino.* I swear. I just..." He took a deep breath, his gray brows drawing together as his expression turned earnest. "I swear to you, *sobrino*, I wanted to tell you the whole truth so many times since you've been here, but it never seemed like the right moment." He reached out to take Carlos's arm, but Carlos pulled away. Hugo flinched, his hand falling back to his side. "I understand how upset you must be."

"Do you? I don't think so, Uncle." Betrayal seared inside him, hotter by the second. His hands and knees trembled and his throat dried, making his voice rough. "Because I trusted you. I trusted you, and you lied to me. I thought I had finally found something real here, something true, but no. Lies. All lies."

He stood and slapped money down on the bar top. He'd never paid in Encanteri before, but now it felt like a necessity. He refused to be beholden to his uncle anymore. First Isabella and now this. It was too much. "I need some air."

"Wait!" Hugo grabbed his wrist. "You don't know how much your father suffered after your mother left. He was distraught. He argued with our parents continuously. He loved your mother and wanted to go to Cuba to find her." His uncle took a breath. "But times were different then, and our parents had both our futures planned out for us. College, then a job at the law firm where our father worked. There was no room for a baby. No room for deviation from the plan."

A muscle ticked in Carlos's cheek as he gritted his teeth. *Leave. Don't stay and listen. Don't let him defend the indefensible.* But in the end, Carlos stayed rooted to the spot, arms crossed and shields up. He needed to know the truth, once and for all. "Go on."

"He never dated, your father. Not in college, not after he graduated. Always pining away for your mother. He tried to contact to her, tried to find her in Cuba, but things with the government there were not good, and after what you told me about your mother's family, I don't think they would've let her talk to him anyway, so…"

"And that makes it okay?" Carlos wasn't feeling particularly charitable to any of them, least of all Hugo. The news was still too new and raw and painful. "He just gave up then?"

"No. He never gave up, *sobrino.*" Hugo met his gaze direct. "Never. Even after years of nothing, even after he finally met someone else and got married at forty. Even then, he never forgot. He used to talk to me about her. He'd come in here to the bar and we'd sit for hours, reminiscing. He still loved your mother even then."

Those words pricked his emotions, letting all the air out of the balloon of Carlos's anger and resentment. He slumped back down on his stool again, deflated and defeated. "I don't understand."

"After our parents died," Hugo said quietly, frowning as he fiddled with a napkin on the bar, "Alejandro and I went through our parents' house to clear it out before selling it. That's when I found the letters. The ones from your mother." He sighed. "Part of me wishes I had said something to your father then, about you. But it had taken him so long to finally find some small happiness after your mother that I couldn't destroy it for him, so I hid the letters away again." Hugo swallowed hard, his bushy gray brows drawing tighter together. "If I'd known he would pass away, too, such a short time later, I would have told him, Carlos. I swear to you I would have told Alejandro."

Carlos let that confession hang there a moment, feeling oddly numb. "But you didn't."

"No. I didn't." Hugo's voice grew gruffer, each word dripping with emotion. "Your father was a good man, a decent man, who would have loved you with his whole heart, just as he loved your mother. How he felt things, his emotions, were too big for this world, I think. That's why they killed him so young. Too young." His breath caught, and despite the animosity of earlier, Carlos couldn't help comforting his uncle, reaching over and placing a hand on Hugo's forearm. "But I always remembered you, *sobrino.* When I received the first letter from you after your mother passed, it felt like *destino.* Fate."

Fate. Carlos snorted. He and fate weren't exactly on the best terms right now. Seemed every time something good came into his life, fate took it away again. The move here. The fresh start. The fling with Isabella. The baby. Hugo. Everything seemed so up in the air and out of reach now.

But he didn't want to give up. He wasn't a quitter by nature. Maybe Hugo had been right at the beginning. Maybe it just wasn't meant to be, and he should let it go. He felt torn and twisted in the worst way. Carlos exhaled slow, then stood again. This time, his uncle let him.

"Are we okay?" Hugo asked. "Can you forgive me?"

"I… I can," Carlos said at last. "Not yet. Not tonight. But soon. I need time to think all this over."

Then he walked out into the cool Barcelona evening, feeling more lost and alone than he ever had before, hoping to find a way to ground himself again and find a new path forward.

CHAPTER ELEVEN

TWO DAYS LATER, *stir-crazy* didn't begin to describe Isabella in her flat. She wasn't used to having this much time off, and it drove her a bit batty. She'd cleaned everything she could clean about a thousand times, drunk tea, read books, watched streaming shows she'd let pile up on TV. But nothing eased the emptiness inside her.

She felt bad about the way she'd left things with Carlos. And she didn't know how to fix it. But all this stewing it over in her head wasn't getting her anywhere close to a solution, so she took a walk on the beach. The water and waves called to her as they always did, the smells of sand and sea bright in her nose. Isabella sat on the shore, watching a group of young surfers catching waves she would've been all over a few months ago, but now things had changed. She'd changed. And not just because of the baby.

Because of Carlos, too. He'd changed her, without her even realizing it.

And that's what scared her the most.

Up until she'd met him, Isabella had been living her life, taking risks, enjoying her freedom. Then he'd come along and made her wish for closeness and companionship and… well, love. She shuddered despite the warm temperatures and wrapped her arms tighter around herself. God. After years of cloying, enforced closeness with her siblings, of looking out for and serving everyone else's needs, the last thing she'd ever expected to crave this late in life was someone to care for. Not just care for. Love.

Isabella sighed and stood, brushing sand off the back of her shorts as seagulls cawed overhead and the brightly colored kites high in the sky caught her eye.

She loved Carlos Martinez, and she had no idea what to do about that.

Distracted and deep in thought, Isabella began to walk, not toward her flat just a few blocks away, but instead in the opposite direction. She wasn't even aware of where she was going until she ended up in front of St.

Aelina's. Isabella stared up at the place and sighed. Seemed even on her time off, she couldn't get away from the place. Oh, well. She needed to talk to her brother Diego, and he was working today, so… The conversation was bound to happen, since he knew about the baby, so she might as well get it over with, considering she was feeling depressed anyway.

After taking the elevator up the floor he was making rounds on, according to the front desk, Isabella waited until Diego emerged from a patient's room, then followed him down the hall to an empty conference room.

Am I ready to do this?

No, not really. But it was too late now, so she summoned her courage and took a seat at the table while he closed the door behind them.

Silly, right? I'm a grown woman making my own choices. I don't need anyone's approval or opinions, yet I'm nervous as hell.

Diego answered right away, scowling. "Isabella? What's wrong?"

She bit her lip and looked away. "Nothing's wrong. I thought I'd stop by and say hello."

He sighed and stepped aside to let her in. The place looked like any other conference room she'd ever seen, beige and boring. A couple of windows let in some natural light, at least. She glanced around then back at him. "How's Grace?"

"Away," he said, waving her off when she raised a brow at him. "Visiting her aunt in Cornwall."

Hmm. Based on his gruff tone and dark expression, she sensed trouble in paradise but didn't dare ask. She wasn't the only Rivas who liked their privacy.

Diego took a seat beside Isabella and rested an elbow on the table, his expression concerned. "How's your head?"

"Still there," Isabella said, her attempt at humor falling flat in the face of her brother's serious look. "It's better. Thank you."

He nodded, then looked away. "I'm worried about you, sis."

Now she frowned. "What? Why?"

His sideways glance said everything.

"Right." She took a deep breath, staring down at her lap. "I was going to tell you about the baby. I just wanted to find the right time."

"Are you going to marry him?"

"What? No." She shook that off, along with the involuntary thrill that went through her at those words. *Do I want to marry Car-*

los? Even if she did, it wasn't like he'd asked. Probably wouldn't now, either, given how they'd left things. Her chest burned a little more. She covered the discomfort by deflecting back to Diego, keeping her voice as calm as possible to hide her growing turmoil inside. "Why would you think that?"

"Well, one, because I've noticed how happy and content you've seemed the past couple of weeks. Never occurred to me why until I confronted him in the hallway."

She bristled, even as she realized he was right. "About that. Don't gang up on Carlos. He's a good man."

"He'd better be, if he's going to marry my sister."

"Stop saying that!" She stood to pace the room, nervous energy scattering inside her like bocce balls. "We're not getting married." She took a deep breath. "Honestly, I'm not even sure if he even likes me anymore after the fight we had."

Diego watched her a moment, then cursed under his breath before raking a hand through his hair. "Look, I'm sorry for how I handled things with him. I was just shocked and scared for you, and then when he said that you were pregnant with his baby, I..." He shook his head and stared out the windows. "I lost it. And I'm sorry."

She walked over and sat down again. "I'm sorry, too. I should have told you about the baby sooner. You shouldn't have found out that way." Isabella let her head fall back to stare at the ceiling. "Have you told the others yet?"

"No. Not yet." He mirrored her position, the same way they used to when they were kids. Shoulder to shoulder, heart to heart. Man, she'd really missed her family since they'd all gone their separate ways, even though they drove her crazy sometimes, too. Diego snorted. "I figured that one's on you. Let you take the heat."

"Gee, thanks." Isabella chuckled. Keeping a secret in the Rivas family was tantamount to treason. She'd get more than an earful from her siblings when the news finally broke.

"You know," Diego said, rolling his head to look at her, "we all give you a hard time, but really we all just love you and want the best for you, Isabella. We adore our *germana gran*."

She had to pinch him for that one, dammit. Even though *germana gran* was Catalan for "older sister," it made her feel ancient, so of course Diego had called her that every chance he got growing up. Such a pain, but she loved him anyway. He laughed and slapped her hand away, and just like that, they were back to being teenagers again, all the cares and fears of adulthood falling away, if only briefly.

"Remember the night of Frida's high school graduation? I made a cake that didn't turn out well at all and you guys still ate it?" Isabella laughed until her sides shook. "Only to find out later that I'd switched the sugar for salt."

"Yes! God, that was awful." Diego shook his head, his eyes watering from laughter. "Still wary of cake because of it. Had a hell of a time picking one out for our wedding."

"I bet." She sighed, sobering as old pain and nostalgia overwhelmed her, making her eyes sting. "Those were good days. When we were still together, before you all moved on."

That must've come out far sadder than she'd intended, because Diego frowned at her once more. "What do you mean?"

She shrugged, trying to play it off, even as her chest squeezed with old sadness. "Nothing. Seriously. Forget I said it."

"No." He met her gaze. "What did you mean by that, Isabella?"

She hadn't meant to get into all this, but… well, everything else was messed up in her world at present, why not this, too? "I don't know. It just seemed like after all those years together, of my taking care of you guys, you all just moved on and left me behind."

The words tumbled out, messy and chaotic, mirroring her emotions.

"Oh, Issy. That's not true at all." He ducked his head to catch her eye, same as he used to do growing up, and her heart pinched a little harder. "Seriously. We all knew how much you worked and sacrificed for us, and we decided that we'd all try to move out as fast as we could to give you your life back. You deserved to live as much as we did, Issy. That's why we left. Not to leave you behind. Never that."

Isabella blinked up at him, stunned.

"And then once you got going, you did so well for yourself on your own that we figured you liked it that way, so we kept our distance." He glanced at the windows again, then back to her. "I even worried about taking the job here at St. Aelina's because I didn't want to cramp your style and make you mad at me."

Oh, God. She straightened fast, knocking Diego aside. "Is that true?"

"*Si.* Of course." He returned to scowling again. "Is that not what you felt?"

"No. Not at all!" She shook her head, scooting around the face him. "I thought you wanted to keep your distance from me, that you were all sick of spending time with me. Oh, God." She covered her face. "We've wasted so much time on silly misunderstandings."

He hugged her then, and they both just soaked in the moment.

When Isabella finally pulled back, she felt like a huge weight had been lifted off her. "Let's not do that again. The whole miscommunication thing, okay?"

"Agreed." He took a deep breath then stared down at his hands. "I wish all problems were solved so easily."

"Me, too." She couldn't stop thinking about Carlos. How she'd messed things up with him, how she wanted to apologize now, but wasn't sure how without making things worse.

"When are you due?" Diego asked, his dark brows knitting.

Isabella flinched a little. She'd been so wrapped up in her own problems, she hadn't even thought about how many times Diego and Grace had tried to conceive and how she'd miscarried three times already. They'd been married five years and still no children, even though both wanted them very much. She sighed and reached over to place her hand over her brother's. "January."

"Wow." Diego looked up then, his smile warm and genuine. "Guess I better learn how to be a great uncle by then, huh? First time and all."

"Yes." She leaned in and hugged him again, just because it felt so good to have her family back. "But you'll already be the best uncle ever. And don't tell Eduardo or Luis I said that. I'll never hear the end of it."

Diego laughed then kissed her cheek. "Promise."

She started to get up but stopped when her brother took her wrist gently.

"Wait," he said, pulling her back into her seat. "What about this man? The baby's father."

Isabella hung her head, smoothing a hand down the front of her shirt. She barely had a bump yet, but she couldn't help imagining what the child would look like. If it would have her eyes and Carlos's nose. Or his hair and her smile. Whatever way it came out, she'd love their child completely.

She shrugged. "What about him?"

"Does he want to marry you? Be with you and the child?" Diego asked, watching her closely.

Isabella sighed. "He does. At least, I think he does. He says he'll be there for us, whatever we need, but…"

"But what?"

"I don't know." She put her head back and covered her face, her throat burning. After a moment, she shook her head and dropped her hands. "I'm scared, Diego."

Her brother frowned and sat up. "Scared? Why? Has he hurt you? Because if he has, I'll—"

"No!" Isabella grabbed him by the shoulders, the same way she used to when they were kids and Diego got angry at one of the neighborhood bullies and threatened to beat them up. "No. God, no. Listen, Carlos is a good man. The best man. He's kind and smart and funny and sweet, and he'd never, ever hurt me like that. Ever. I trust him completely."

It wasn't until those words left her mouth that she realized they were true. She did trust

Carlos. The problem was trusting herself. "I just…" She looked away, searching for the words to explain the knot of tension inside her. "I'm scared of being trapped again."

"Trapped?" Diego tilted his head, his expression confused.

"Like when we were kids. Mom passed away, then Dad got sick, and I had no choice but to step up and take over, because otherwise they would have split up our family. I did what I had to do." Guilt squeezed her gut, making her wince. "Not that I resented helping out, but…"

"But it wasn't what you would've chosen for yourself." Diego nodded. "I understand, Isabella. You were just a child yourself. It's an awful burden to put on someone so young. Please don't feel guilty about that."

"I don't…" she started to say, but he raised a dark brow at her, and she snorted. Diego had always been a good reader of people. Probably why he made such a fantastic doctor now. "Okay. Yes. I've been carrying around some guilt about that. But it's like, over the years, it's become who I am. The guilt. The need for freedom. The independence." Isabella lifted a shoulder, fiddling with the hem of her shirt. "What if I'm with Carlos and I lose myself again? What if something happens and I must take charge? What if we get married and it doesn't work out?"

Diego waited a beat or two, then straightened, taking her hands again. "None of us knows what tomorrow will bring, Issy. That's the beauty and horror of life. All we can do is seize what's right in front of us, take the joy where we find it. The love. And cherish it with all our hearts." He met and held her gaze. "If this Carlos is half as wonderful as you think he is, my guess is he'll stand by you no matter what. Through thick and thin. That's what marriage is. Not a trap. Not even a cage. It's a framework of commitment and trust. One you build together to withstand the good times and bad. One that supports both of you when you need it most. If you can find that with Carlos, sister, then you should hold on tight and never let go."

"What if I'm too late?"

Her brother laughed. "Based on what I saw in the ER, he's so far gone over you, Issy, he's still reeling over all this. If you don't wait forever, I'm sure you can fix things."

Isabella hugged him tight, then pulled back, smiling. "When did you get so smart?"

"Well, if you ask Grace, I've still got a long

way to go." He gave a sad little chuckle, then stood before she could ask him any more about it. "Now, let's talk about how exactly you're going to win this man of yours back."

CHAPTER TWELVE

THE NEXT MORNING, Carlos woke up determined. He'd barely slept the night before, tossing and turning, trying to find a resolution that would make everyone happy and failing miserably. Not to mention the things his uncle had told him about his father.

His whole life, Carlos had believed that his biological father didn't want him, but now he knew differently. He was unsure how to feel about that yet. Part of him felt happy, overjoyed, to know that there wasn't something wrong with him, some defect that made him unworthy and unlovable. But the other part of him felt fury. All the lies, the deception, the hidden secrets.

Bah! He'd had enough of those to last more than a lifetime.

Grumbling, he rolled out of bed and headed for the bathroom. After a brisk shower and shave, he pulled out a fresh pair of jeans and a T-shirt from his closet and put them on before padding barefoot to the kitchen to start a pot of coffee. More caffeine needed.

He was scheduled to work the night shift at the ER later but had the rest of the day free. For the best, since he had a lot of thinking to do. He checked his emails and waited for the coffee maker to ding, then fixed his mug and had a seat at the small dining room table, head full and heart aching.

Hard to keep his two problems separate, no matter how he tried to work out one issue at a time. The breakup with Isabella had been bad. Very bad. The way they'd left things felt undefined and raw, and he didn't like it. He still wanted more than anything to be there for her, to be with her, but she'd stated clearly that she didn't want him crowding into her life. Maybe he should just accept that and move on. Given the state of technology, there were many ways to stay connected to people you cared for without living with them. They could call or text or FaceTime. He could continue to be a part of their baby's life no matter how things ended up between him and Isabella.

Deep down, though, Carlos knew that wasn't enough for him. Would never be enough.

Which brought his own situation and those letters right back to the top of his mind. How could Hugo have hidden that from him? From his father? Worse, how could their parents not have told Alejandro and Hugo the truth before it was too late? Before Carlos had spent his whole life believing he was an unwanted bastard from Cuba? Even now, those words were a gut punch to him.

He drank more coffee and stared at the wall across from him as new realizations came to light. Honestly, Uncle Hugo hadn't been the only one who'd kept secrets. Carlos had never shared with him or anyone else the humiliating things he'd suffered growing up. Not even his mother. She'd been through enough because of his father. She didn't need to know that her son was getting attacked because of it, too. But Cuba was very different than Barcelona, and unwed mothers something to be pitied and looked down on there. But being called names, beaten up and bullied by the other kids in his neighborhood in Havana because of his parentage had taught him the benefit of being likable, of being easygoing and affable and kind. Other kids didn't punch you so hard if you were funny or did nice things for them. So, he'd learned to deal with things the best way he could.

God. So many years. So many wasted years.

He scrubbed a hand over his face, feeling bleary despite the caffeine. After a deep breath, he sat back. The walls seemed to be closing in on him now. Everywhere he looked in the flat, all he could picture was Isabella. The sofa where she'd sat the first night to look at his mother's old diaries. The table where they'd gone over pictures and places for their tour of the city. The bedroom where she'd stayed after he'd brought her home from the hospital, where they'd fought, where they'd ended things for good…

No. He needed to get out, get some fresh air, get some new ideas of how to fix this into his head.

Carlos dumped the rest of his coffee down the drain and rinsed out the cup before setting it in the holder beside the sink to dry. He shoved his feet into some shoes, then grabbed his keys and headed out for a walk. He wandered without really thinking about it, past buildings and tourists and vendors, ending up down by the beach again. Even here, he saw Isabella everywhere. The place where they'd saved that man with the heart attack. The restaurant where they'd shared their first meal. The spot where they'd decided to keep the night going and headed back to her place.

Chest tight and temples throbbing, he plunked down on a bench and stared at the horizon. He loved her. Plain and simple. He loved Isabella Rivas, and he loved their baby. But they didn't love him back. Not enough to want to be with him. So…what?

Let them go.

He flinched. No. He didn't want to give up. Didn't want to let go. That would only repeat the mistakes that had happened to him. He would never desert his own child. Never.

A sea breeze blew, ruffling his hair and cooling his heated skin. But he didn't want to force himself on Isabella, either. Didn't want to go against her wishes. That would be no better than the other idea.

He closed his eyes and hung his head again, allowing the conversation with his uncle the night before to replay in his head. Truthfully, he felt a bit guilty about how that conversation had ended. The way he'd spoken to his uncle. He'd been angry, yes, and rightfully so for the things that were kept from him. But the more he thought about it, the more Carlos could understand why his uncle had hidden the letter from his father. Hugo had cared for his younger brother and he'd wanted to protect him, no matter how misguided his actions might have been. So, no. Carlos didn't blame his uncle. Not really. If he wanted to be upset with someone, it should be the parents, his grandparents. On both sides. They were the real villains here. But they were all long dead, so that did him no good, either.

At his core, Carlos knew the healthiest thing to do would be to let it go and start fresh. Easier said than done. He snorted. God, how many times had he talked to patients and given them that advice? He was lucky they hadn't told him where to get off, even if the advice came from a good place.

Difficult to listen to the tiny voice inside your soul, for sure.

He sat there awhile longer, going in circles in his head without really reaching a conclusion before finally heading back to his flat. Maybe he'd clean or take a nap or something to use up the time before his shift, because if he kept thinking in circles like this, it would drive him nuts. Then, about half a block from his place, it hit him. The thing to do to help him get out of this mess. His original reason for coming to Barcelona in the first place.

The diaries.

He went back up to the flat and grabbed his mother's book. Maybe if he retraced the steps of their final moments together one more time, it would help him gain clarity over the past and the present now. Maybe find some context in those final entries that would apply to his current situation. He walked out and jogged down the stairs with the book under his arm—only to nearly crash into Uncle Hugo on the sidewalk.

They both stood, warily eyeing the other, uncomfortable together for the first time.

Finally, Hugo cleared his throat and frowned down at the sidewalk. "*Mi sobrino.*"

"*Tío.*"

"I…uh…" his uncle started, then shook his head. "I want you to know how sorry I am about everything, Carlos. I never meant to hurt you."

"I know," he said, and meant it. But he still felt torn up inside and wasn't ready to go back to normal just yet. He edged past his uncle and pointed vaguely in the direction he was headed, holding up his mother's diary. "I'm on my way to Parc del Laberint d'Horta. Figured I'd visit the last place where my parents saw each other. Seems fitting."

Hugo looked up at him and gave a curt nod, a moment passing between the two men. Not forgiveness, because Carlos had already forgiven his uncle, even if he hadn't forgotten the pain yet. More of an understanding. They knew each other now, on a deeper level, the good and the bad, and they were okay. Or they would be, soon. Once Carlos got his current knot of a problem straightened out. "I hope you find what you are looking for."

"Me, too, *Tío*. Me, too," Carlos said, giving his uncle a small, sad smile before turning and walking away.

Isabella stood on the doorstep of Carlos's flat two hours later and took a deep breath, running through the coaching session she'd had with her brother Diego the day before. *Tell the truth. Listen to what he has to say. Compromise. If you love him, you'll work it out. That's what love is. Not a trap but a framework to build on together.*

Her hand trembled slightly as she knocked on the door, then smoothed that same hand down the front of her yellow sundress. The same dress she'd worn when they'd toured the city together. Carlos had told her how much he liked that color on her, and it had significance for her because she'd also been wearing it that night when they'd shared their first kiss. Well, their first kiss after the fling—their first kiss when it really counted.

She waited. Waited some more. Nothing.

Huh. Isabella knocked again. She'd checked the roster at St. Aelina's earlier when she'd checked in with Mario about her first shift back after release, and Carlos wasn't scheduled to work until that night, so… Maybe he went grocery shopping. Or for a walk around the city.

Or for a date with someone else already.

No. She scowled. Given how busy they both were, time wasn't on their side when it came to a social life. Probably why lots of people in the medical profession ended up dating other medical people. Besides, Carlos didn't go from one relationship to another without a thought or care. He wasn't the type. He felt deeply. One of the things she loved most about him.

So, then. Where had he gone?

Isabella knocked once more time with no response before she headed downstairs to the bar. If Carlos was out, she'd leave a note with his uncle asking him to call her when he could. No pressure, just opening those lines of communication again between them after she'd severed them so brutally a few nights earlier. She managed not to cringe at that last regretful thought—barely.

Even at lunchtime, patrons filled Encanteri to capacity. She sidled past a group of tourists waiting for a table near the entrance and headed through the packed interior toward the bar. Carlos's uncle was helping mix drinks and deliver food, bustling around the place like a man half his age, chatting and laughing with customers.

At least until he saw Isabella and froze, his expression changing from happy to guarded in seconds. Nervous, she fidgeted near the bar while he finished with a table of guests before finally making his way back to her.

"*Hola,*" he said, his tone much cooler than their previous exchanges. "What can I get you?"

"I hoped to speak with Carlos," Isabella said past her tight vocal cords. "Will he be back soon?"

"I'm not sure." Hugo fiddled with some bottles and taps, not meeting her gaze. "Does he want to see you?"

Yikes. The bluntness of his question smacked her hard in the heart. And honestly, she wasn't sure. Her dismay must've shown on her face, though she tried to hide it, because Hugo cursed softly, then set a glass of sparkling water in front of her. "I know something is going on between you two. He didn't tell me specifics, just that you turned him away, Isabella. You hurt my nephew, badly. I don't like it when people I love are hurting."

"I know," she said, blinking hard against the sting in her eyes. She didn't want to cry now. She'd done enough of that already the past two days. And this was too important for tears. She had to get this right. "And I'm so very sorry for hurting Carlos. It was never my intention to do so. He's the most wonderful man I've ever known. But I'm scared."

"Of him?" Hugo gave her a confused look, his bushy gray brows knit.

"Of everything." She took a sip of her water, grateful for its coolness on her parched throat. "I'm not sure how much you and Carlos have talked about me."

"Some," he said, giving her a kind smile, so like his nephew's. "I know that you had a hard time growing up. You are a strong woman. That strength is not forged from happiness."

"No, it's not." She laughed softly, shaking her head as she stared down into her glass. "This whole thing with Carlos—it all happened so fast, and I panicked and…" She sighed and glanced up at Hugo. "I'm afraid I didn't handle it very well at all. I'm not used to having other people to depend on during difficulties."

"I understand." Hugo patted her hand atop the bar. "I am an older sibling, too."

"Oh," she said, then when that sank in, she looked up at him. "Oh."

"*Si.*" Hugo sighed and came around the bar to sit on the stool beside hers. "My nephew and I, we had some issues, too, last night. I shared some things with him about his father that I should have told him long ago. It's hard, isn't it? Keeping secrets."

"*Si.* It is." She turned slightly to face him. "That's how misunderstandings occur. My younger brother and I had a similar talk, about things that happened that I had interpreted one way, but my siblings had meant in a totally different way." She gave a sad little snort. "Communication is hard."

"It is. Necessary, too." He narrowed his gaze on her. "How are you?"

She considered telling him about the baby,

but no. Carlos should be the one to share that with his uncle. The sooner the better. Because the time for keeping silent about the pregnancy had long passed, and Isabella found she didn't want to stay quiet anymore. She wasn't scared now—at least not as much as she had been, anyway.

"Good. Sad and lonely, but good." She took a deep breath, frowning down at her hands in her lap. "I really am sorry about hurting Carlos. It was wrong of me to walk away. I regret that now, more than I can say. But I do love your nephew, more than I ever thought possible, and I want to make it up to him, if he'll let me."

Hugo's smile increased to a grin. "*Lloeu Jesús. L'amor jove guanya al final!*"

Praise Jesus. Young love wins in the end.

His voice boomed through the already boisterous bar, loud enough for table nearby to turn and look at them. Heat prickled Isabella's cheeks as Hugo pulled her off her stool and into a bear hug. Shock froze her in place for a moment before, finally, she laughed, too, and hugged him back.

All this openness, this vulnerability, felt amazing—if still a bit terrifying.

Maybe that's how true freedom was. The

same rush of the waves, the same quickening of her heart she felt surfing a huge curl, only now her feet were firmly planted on the ground and without a beach in sight.

"Right." Hugo released her at last. "You must go to Carlos and tell him how you feel."

"Where is he?" Apprehension and anticipation sizzled through her veins in equal measure.

"Parc del Laberint d'Horta." Hugo winked. "Have you been there?"

"*Si.*" She clenched her fists, hoping to dispel some of the nervous energy fizzing inside her. "We went there together, with the diary." Everything came full circle now and she had to go, to go to Carlos to say her apologies and make him see how much she loved him and wanted to be with him, whatever that looked like for them. She saw her future, and it was Carlos. Carlos and their baby. After a quick kiss on Hugo's cheek, Isabella hurried toward the door. "Wish me luck, Hugo."

"*Molta sort, carinyo!*" he called after her, waving. "*Molta sort.*"

CHAPTER THIRTEEN

THE CLOCKS HAD struck noon by the time Carlos stepped off the Metro from Sant Marti and walked across the plaza to the Parc del Laberint d'Horta. Admission was free on Wednesdays, so even midweek, lots of people and tourists milled about. Bright sunshine lit the area, and the blue skies above reflected in the small pools he passed near the entrance before heading down a shady tree-lined gravel path, not seeking anywhere in particular.

Being outside, in nature, soothed him and helped calm his mind. As he wandered, Carlos opened the diary and read several pages of his mother's writing. About meeting his father for the first time while visiting La Sagrada Familia. Seeing someone across a crowded room and knowing they were the one.

Carlos took a deep breath and continued

walking. Thinking back on that first evening on the beach with Isabella, he'd kind of felt the same. The same tug of recognition, the same pull of inevitability that this person would be important to him in his life. At the time, he'd tried to write it off as infatuation, as lust, since they'd made love for the first time that same night. But now, looking back, he could see that, no. It wasn't just a fling. It had been love. Even then. For that's the night they'd conceived their child together.

He walked down a flight of steps and continued past several stone buildings and statuary before coming to the large reflecting pool. Many tourists stopped here, sitting on the short walls surrounding the pool or cooing to their children in strollers. Carlos smiled. Perhaps someday, that would be him and Isabella with their child. The thought filled him with joy.

His heart still pinched, though, knowing they might not be a couple, but he needed to learn to be okay with whatever happened. Isabella wasn't his father. She wasn't leaving him, because they'd never actually been committed in the first place.

If he had to do it all over again, he would've asked her sooner to be his, he thought. Not marriage, just yet, because his Isabella was gun-shy there, and for good reason after what she'd been through growing up. But he would have pledged himself to her and made sure she knew that he would be there with her through it all, in whatever way worked for her. Maybe if he'd done that, they wouldn't be where they were now, but nothing for it now.

Continuing past the pool, Carlos stopped on a small footbridge overlooking a creek running through the park. Quieter here, the chatter of tourists drowned out by the rush of water beneath the bridge and birdsong above. Here, he thought of Uncle Hugo and their argument. He was ready to forget it now, as he hadn't been earlier. Hugo meant well, but he'd made a mistake. Water under the bridge. Literally.

He stared down into the channel below, diary in his hands, and said a silent prayer to his mother above for wisdom. Help to finally do the right thing with Isabella and break the cycle of the past, of the secrets and lies and hidden things and get it all out in the open at last.

Ahead were the stairs leading down to the maze. Surprisingly, not many people were there yet, and it seemed fitting to get lost in there awhile, to work his way through it as he worked through the tangle of problems and emotions inside him. Uncle Hugo had been right, Carlos realized. He was impulsive, and maybe even reckless in his own way—with his emotions, certainly. He always cared too much, too soon. Allowed his feelings and instincts to lead. Sometimes it turned out well. Other times not. But that was him, and he didn't want to change. Wasn't sure he could at that point.

Carlos liked being on the front lines, helping people, caring for people, making people's lives better. And if that made him impulsive and reckless, then so be it. He'd gladly wear those titles.

The one thing he didn't want, though, was to be reckless and impulsive where Isabella and the baby were concerned. He hesitated, stopping at a corner in the maze, looking this way and that, choosing which path to take. Voices of others, somewhere inside the puzzle, too, echoed around him, but no one else appeared. Only him and his instincts. Diary under his arm, he turned right and continued deeper into the maze, the smell of cedar trees and the crunch of gravel beneath his feet his only companions.

So, how to handle things with Isabella. She feared commitment, feared being trapped again. That's what she'd said. Deep down, he thought, she also feared making a mistake and not being able to change course. Carlos got that. For many years, he'd felt trapped in Cuba, locked into a past he had no control over and a hazy future, at best. Breaking out and coming to Barcelona had been one of the best decisions he'd ever made.

Carlos supposed he could just tell her how he felt and let her decide how to proceed. But part of him feared she might shut him out completely, given how she'd reacted the other night at his flat. Then again, the reckless part of him—the part he'd inherited from his father, according to Uncle Hugo—said he should take the chance, take the risk, because otherwise he'd regret it for the rest of his life.

And if his parents' tumultuous love affair had taught him anything, it was to live with no regrets.

Finally, after what felt like a small eternity, he made another turn and emerged into the center of the maze. Curved stone benches encircled a beautiful statue of Eros, the mischievous god of love. Alone, he took a seat near a towering cedar arch to rest his feet. Set the diary on the bench beside him and turned his face up to the sky, eyes closed and heart open, whispering a prayer for guidance, "*Madre, por favor ayúdame. Dame una señal. Dime que debo hacer.*"

Mother, please help me. Give me a sign. Tell me what I should do.

With tourist crowds, it took Isabella about a half hour to get to the park and through the entrance. The Horta complex itself was huge, though, and other than the visit with Carlos a few weeks earlier, where they'd stuck to the main path to the maze, she hadn't been there for years.

She followed the same path now, trying to put herself in Carlos's mind-set and think where he would go. The maze, obviously, at the center of the park, but there were many routes to get there, some longer than others. Perhaps the best thing she could do was head in that direction, then wait for him. He'd show up eventually, she felt certain.

Isabella started down a shady path to her left, enjoying the break from the heat of the sun beating down on her. She'd healed well from her concussion and really the only thing she noticed now, other than the bruise, was a slight twinge near her temple occasionally. But otherwise, her dizziness had gone, as had the fogginess in her brain. She felt clear again, finally, and wanted to take advantage of that today with Carlos.

Clear. Such a glorious word.

Truthfully, she hadn't realized how many misconceptions she'd held about herself, about her family, for so long. Diego had set her straight, thankfully, but how many years had she lost, years she could've spent with her family, being close to them, sharing their lives, if only she'd spoken up about how she really felt, and they'd done the same? The lesson wasn't lost on her. And she refused to move forward with the same mind-set that had gotten her here. Time for new thinking, a fresh start. One that would include Carlos and their child, together, if things went well today.

After talking with her brother yesterday and then Hugo today, Isabella knew deep inside that Carlos was her person. She loved him, more than she'd ever thought possible, and she wanted to spend forever with him if he'd forgive her. She'd said and done some awful things, and it hurt remembering him walking away from her that night, but she needed to be strong now. She realized love wasn't a cage. Love wasn't a trap. Love truly set you free.

Giving yourself fully to another person and having them do the same to you.

Vulnerability was the only freedom, really.

Now, she just needed to find Carlos.

Isabella continued down the path and emerged into Lion Square. She remembered coming here with her parents when she'd been maybe three years old. One of her first memories. Her mother, pregnant with Eduardo at the time, had pushed baby Diego in a stroller. She'd been so happy, laughing and pointing out things to little Isabella. Her father holding her hand, buying her a bag of bread crumbs to feed the birds, getting her lemon gelato to eat as they walked through the park. Those had been such happy times, before it all went wrong.

Instead of feeling sad or burdened remembering, as she had in the past, she felt hopeful and grateful. Wishing one day to build such happy times with her own child and Carlos. Maybe they would bring the baby here, show them the gardens, feed the pigeons. She passed a small fountain and spotted a young mother doing much the same with her toddler. Yes, that would be very nice indeed. Isabella smiled at the woman and her child as she passed.

She stepped out of Lion Square, a warm breeze stirring her skirt around her legs, taking the long way around and stopping at the bosket and the Minotaur's Grotto. So beautiful, so serene. She wished Carlos could be there to enjoy it with her. Maybe next time. *Please, God. Let there be a next time.* Isabella walked onward toward the romantic channel and took the small stone footbridge over it. Stopped to make another silent wish that things would work out for them well in the end, then continued over to the neo-classical pavilion and the large reflecting pool there in front of the fountain of nymph Egeria.

Isabella stopped and closed her eyes, letting the gentle gurgling sound of water surround her, calming her rapid pulse and easing away the last ripple of her nervousness. A sense of rightness filled her. She wanted to be with Carlos, make a life with him, a future with him. *Now's the time.*

After a deep breath for courage, she crossed back over the bridge and headed into the maze at last. So peaceful and quiet there, but she kept moving at a brisk pace. If Carlos had arrived here before her, she didn't want to miss him. As was usual, though, she got lost, turning corner after corner only to find another dead end or another path to follow. A story spread among the locals said once upon a time a newly married young couple had gotten lost in the maze with their young baby. When they finally found their way out again, their child was an adult. She hoped it wouldn't take her that long to find her happily-ever-after with the man she loved.

Time lost meaning in there among the green cedars and the short shadows cast by the sun as it passed overhead, the heat of it prickling her bare shoulders. Eventually she made a final turn and stopped cold.

Carlos sat on a stone bench in the innermost circle of the maze, head bowed and his mother's diary open on his lap as he read. His tousled dark hair gleamed almost midnight blue beneath the bright sunshine, and he looked so handsome her heart skipped a beat.

She hesitated, wanting to run and throw herself into his arms and wanting to hide all at the same time, but then he looked up and their gazes met, and it seemed all the oxygen in the world evaporated. She opened her mouth, closed it, then bit her lips as she put one foot in front of the other toward him, knowing this would be the most important journey she'd ever make in her life, stopping only when she stood in front of him.

He blinked up at her shielding his eyes with his hand. "Isabella."

"Carlos."

All the things she'd planned to say vanished from her head and she panicked, ending up taking a seat on the bench beside him, almost touching but not quite.

The air between them seemed electrified with possibilities.

"I went—" she started at the same time he said, "I talked—"

They both laughed, and a bit of the tension eased.

"Please, you go first," he said to her.

"No, no, you." Isabella swallowed hard, not knowing what to do with her hands, at last clasping them in her lap so he wouldn't see how much she shook. Not from fear, but from anticipation. This close she could see the hint of stubble already forming on his chiseled jaw, smell his spicy aftershave and the hint of soap and sweat mixed in, hear the catch in his breath, as if he felt nervous, too. They hadn't known each other that long, really, and yet it felt like they'd been a part of each other forever. Isabella never wanted to let him go again. “Please.”

Carlos nodded, then cleared his throat, closing the diary and holding it on his lap, his gaze locked on the Eros statue before them as he swallowed hard, the sleek muscles in his tanned throat working. “I talked to my uncle Hugo after you left the other night. Found out some things about my parents I didn't know.”

His dark brows twitched together in a brief frown, and he dropped his gaze to his toes. “The letters my mother sent to my father, telling him about me. He never received them, apparently. Uncle Hugo said their parents hid them from him, so he never knew he had a son. Hugo said my father spent years pining after my mother, trying to find her, but things with Cuba were not good then, and he never saw her again. Later, after their parents died, Hugo found the letters, but he decided not to show them to my father even then. Because he'd finally moved on, gotten married, found happiness, so he hid them again. Then my father got sick and died, never knowing about me.”

“Oh, Carlos.” Isabella reached over then, placing her hand over his, aching for him. “I'm so very sorry. That's terrible. But at least you know now that he loved your mother, that he didn't stop looking for her. That if he'd known about you, he would have loved you, too."

He nodded. A beat passed, then two, his skin warm under hers. Her eyes stinging with tears over all the time he'd lost, over the father he never got to meet.

She sighed. "I went to see my brother Diego the day after I left your flat. We talked about growing up, about how I felt like they'd all left me behind and moved on without me after I'd done everything for them." She gave a sad little snort and shook her head. "Turns out I was wrong. My siblings didn't leave me behind at all. They talked and decided to get out of the house as soon as they could so I could finally have a life of my own. They did it for me." She sniffled, the tears falling anyway, despite her wishes. She looked up to the blue skies above, the sun slipping behind a puffy white cloud. "God, can you believe it? All that time, all those years, I thought they didn't care. I kept my distance, thinking I'd protected myself, my freedom, but it trapped me in misbelief."

"Oh, *hermosa*." Carlos shifted slightly, moving closer to slip his arm around her shoulders and pull her into his side. "We've both wasted so much time, kept so much hidden inside, waiting, watching." He took a breath, then kissed the top of her head, tucked under his chin. "I don't want to wait anymore."

"Me neither," she said, perfectly content tucked against him. "I've never been as happy as I have been with you. From that first night on the beach to now, you've shown me what a wonderful man you are. Kind, compassionate, caring. Everything I want in a man, a partner. After spending those years caring for my father and my siblings, I thought love was a trap. I closed in on myself for protection, pushing everyone away. But meeting you allowed me to be vulnerable, showed me that things could be different, if I dared to take a chance with you.

"I want to take that chance with you, Carlos. I want a relationship with you. I want to rebuild connections with my family. I want to tell everyone who'll listen about our baby." She pulled away enough to look into his gorgeous dark eyes and said what she needed to say, no matter how scary. "I want a life with you, Carlos. I love you."

He smiled, and the sun broke though again

above. Then he kissed her, and warmth burst forth like fireworks inside her. Isabella wrapped her arms around his neck and pulled him closer, opening to him as he deepened the kiss, sweeping his tongue into her mouth, his arms going around her waist, holding her close, body to body, heart to heart, as Eros looked down on them and smiled.

When Carlos finally pulled back, they were both breathless and grinning. He rested his forehead against her, not letting her go. "*Hermosa*, I love you, too. I came to Barcelona to trace my parents' story, experience what they did, connect with them as best I could through this place and through my uncle. But I never in a million years expected to start a new story of my own with you, Isabella. With our child." He moved one hand down to rest on her small baby bump, cleverly concealed by her yellow sundress. "I want to be with you, *hermosa*. We can date. I can court you right. And when we're both ready, we can live together, maybe even become engaged. Whatever you want, whenever you want. I just want to be by your side, *cariña*. Now and forever. You are my future. You and our baby."

They kissed again, slow and sweet this

time, pulling back when a few more tourists entered the area and began snapping pictures. Isabella picked up his mother's diary and grinned. "Perhaps we should start a new diary of our own. That way when the baby gets older, we can read our stories to them, and they can keep them as they grow."

"*Si.* I think that's a perfect idea, *hermosa.*" He kissed her quick, then stood and held out his hand. "Shall we go? Together?"

"*Si.*" Isabella took his hand and pushed to her feet, his mother's diary clutched to her chest like a treasure. "I will go anywhere with you, *amor meu. Sempre amb tu.*"

They headed out of the maze together, hand in hand, Carlos whispering in her ear, "*Sempre amb tu.*"

Always with you.

EPILOGUE

Eighteen months later

ISABELLA STOOD OUTSIDE the bar, her baby in her arms, and stared at the sign on the door that read *Cerrado para fiesta privada. Closed for a private party.* A big day. Little Ana Rosa's first birthday. They'd named her after both of their mothers. Hard to believe the time had gone so fast. Isabella felt excited and more than a little self-conscious, since she still carried some of her baby weight and her old clothes didn't quite fit yet.

"What do you think, baby girl, huh?" She kissed the top of her daughter's head, then smoothed a hand over her downy hair. Dark brown and curly like her father's and sticking up all over no matter what Isabella did. Little Ana Rosa was so easygoing, though, just like her *papá*, and Isabella couldn't love either one of them more. "Let's go inside and see him, eh?"

She pulled open the door and walked inside the sparkling-clean bar. Uncle Hugo had made sure the place gleamed from top to bottom for their big event. In fact, the air still smelled like lemon floor polish. Hugo came out of his office in the back and walked over to her, arms open. "*Mi sobrina!*" He kissed Isabella soundly on both cheeks, then took baby Ana Rosa from her. "And how's my *dulce niña* today?" He made a bunch of silly faces, trying to get the baby to laugh. Ana Rosa said something that was supposed to be "Hugo" but came out mainly gibberish. "You are such a good girl, yes, you are. *Tío* Hugo's good little girl."

The sight of the older man coddling their daughter melted Isabella's heart. Impossible not to smile, even though she had to warn him, "Don't jostle her around too much. I fed her before we came. She'll upchuck all over you."

"Well, that's okay, isn't it?" Hugo cooed, beaming down at his grandniece like she was the most wonderful thing in the world. Isabella felt the same way. There'd been a few odd moments when she'd been in labor where she'd worried about what might happen after the birth. It was her first baby, and while she and Carlos were committed to each other and their child, what if she did something wrong? What if the baby never bonded with her? What if she made a horrible mother?

But the moment she'd held tiny, red and squalling Ana Rosa in her arms and the baby had stared up at Isabella with pure wonder, every single one of her fears had fled. They'd formed an unbreakable bond in that moment, never to be severed. The most profound experience Isabella had ever had in her life. The second most profound? Falling in love with Carlos and trusting him. Really trusting him. Not just with words, but with her whole heart and soul. They had a healthy and strong and wonderful relationship, even if they hadn't made it official yet. Someday, it would come. Carlos respected her boundaries, he'd said. And she loved him for that, even if maybe those boundaries had changed and she wanted more.

"*Hermosa!*" Carlos called from the upper balcony and hurried downstairs to kiss her, then take his daughter from Hugo and put her over his shoulder—after another kiss, of course. "When did you get here?"

"Just now," she said, smiling. That seemed to be all she did these days, because she was just so happy. "Why?"

"No reason." Carlos leaned in and quickly kissed her again before leading her over to the bar, which had been decorated with streamers and balloons for the occasion. "The party starts in about an hour, and guests will arrive before that."

They'd invited their friends from work, of course, and Carlos's friends who owned the dance studio. Isabella's siblings, too, who were coming in from all over Spain to help them celebrate the happy day.

Ana Rosa talked animatedly to her father, gurgling and squeaking, happy as a clam. Hugo excused himself and went back into his office to finish up a few things, leaving the three of them alone in the bar.

"Hey," Carlos said to her over their daughter's head. "Before everyone else gets here, there's something I want to ask you."

He looked so serious all of a sudden that her heart skipped a beat.

"Okay," she said, her tone hesitant. "What is it?"

He hiked his chin to a small box on the counter, wrapped in silver paper, partially hidden behind all the decorations and other gifts for their daughter. "Open that one. It's for you, *hermosa*."

"Really?" She frowned and pulled the little box closer. "From whom?"

"From me."

Her fingers trembled slightly, and her pulse raced.

She looked up at him, then back at the box, blinking, tears welling as she opened it to find a sparkling diamond ring inside. "I don't— I didn't expect this at all, *cariño*."

"I know, *hermosa*," he said, smiling. "That's what makes it perfect." Carlos transferred their daughter to his other arm, then whispered, "Will you marry me?"

Isabella laughed, placing her shaking fingers over her mouth, unable to believe that everything she'd ever wanted stood right before her. "*Si.* Yes, of course I will marry you. I love you, Carlos. More than I ever thought possible."

He kissed her then. When they finally pulled apart, nothing could've removed the silly grin from her face. Ana Rosa squealed with delight. Isabella knew exactly how their daughter felt.

Carlos rested his forehead against hers,

his dimples on full display. "Have I told you lately how much I love you?"

"You have, actually," she said, his words so heartfelt and so true and so real, Isabella ached inside, in the best possible way. "And I promise to love you with all my heart for as long as I live, Carlos."

"Same, *hermosa*," Carlos said, kissing her again. "Same."

Ana Rosa became enthralled with the balloons and Isabella thanked her lucky stars for fate bringing Carlos to Barcelona and into her life. And as they laughed and played with their daughter, Isabella felt forever grateful for the transformative power of love and trust. True freedom. She knew that now. And it had made an amazing difference in her life.

* * * * *

If you missed the previous story in the Night Shift in Barcelona quartet, then check out

The Night they Never Forgot
by Scarlet Wilson

And there are two more stories to come Available July 2022!

If you enjoyed this story, check out these other great reads from Traci Douglass

Island Reunion with the Single Dad
Costa Rican Fling with the Doc

All available now!